Hurmence, Belinda

Hu

Tancy

910911

DATE DUE		
OCT 9 1991		
OCT 24 1991		
NOV 6 - 1991		
NOV 20 1991		
JUL 9 - 1992		
SEP - 3 1993		
07		
JUN 1 7 1996		
AUG 0 2 2004		
JUN 0 5 2008		

Tancy

Also by Belinda Hurmence

A Girl Called Boy
Tough Tiffany

Tancy

Belinda Hurmence

CLARION BOOKS
TICKNOR & FIELDS:
A HOUGHTON MIFFLIN COMPANY
NEW YORK

Clarion Books
Ticknor & Fields, a Houghton Mifflin Company

Printed in the U.S.A.

Library of Congress Cataloging in Publication Data
Hurmence, Belinda.
Tancy.
Summary: At the end of the Civil War, a young house
slave on a small North Carolina plantation searches for
her mother who was mysteriously sold when Tancy was a
baby.
[1. Slavery — Fiction.   2. United States — History —
Civil War, 1861–1865 — Fiction]   I. Title.
PZ7.H9567Tan   1984   [Fic]   83-19035
ISBN 0-89919-228-9

S 10 9 8 7 6 5 4 3

For Leslie

Tancy

1

IN THE CUBBY under the hall stairs of the old log house, the slave girl Tancy wept for her dead master.

Tancy's beloved Master Gaither, dead! Just noon last Thursday, he had sat at the table with his son, Billy, the two of them hollering and bragging on their coonhounds, the way they did always when Billy came home from college. As always, once dinner was done, they tramped out to where Stud waited with the horses, to slaughter through the holidays whatever flew, swam, ran, or crept, and to pass back and forth between them Mas Gaither's flask of homemade brandy.

Today, with the Christmas log barely ashes in the parlor fireplace, that hearty outdoorsman lay in his coffin, indoors forever, uncommonly dressed up, dead at age sixty-three of a burst appendix. For Christmas the master had given Tancy a striped ribbon. Before New Year's his wife, the soft, sweet woman he called Puddin, gave her maid the two pennies that had weighted shut her dead husband's eyes.

A ribbon and two pennies. Oh, why did he have to die? Now Tancy had only Miss Puddin left, and if something should happen to her – the very thought shattered the young maid. For the master and Miss Puddin meant everything to Tancy, everything. She had never known a mother or a father.

"Little Tancy," Billy sighed, when he came upon the sorrowing creature huddled beneath the stairs. He put his arms around her and comforted her.

Billy was Tancy's first love, her childhood playmate, the one who had taught her to read. Tancy worshiped him still, but he was not aware of that. He had ignored her ever since a robust fellow from the quarters, Stud, had been given him for a waiting boy. Billy's acknowledgment of their mutual grief on this terrible day overwhelmed Tancy. She sobbed aloud.

"Mustn't cry, Tancy. Be a big girl," Billy advised her gravely. He was, after all, two years older than she, and a university man. "Tancy's growing up." He used her apron to wipe her eyes. "All grown up," he marveled, a new note entering his voice. He touched her shoulder. When she stiffened, he caught her around the waist and pressed her buttocks to himself. "Getting a *nice* little figure," he murmured in a strangled tone.

The first carriageful of mourners arriving saved her. Tancy tore away from him to the kitchen, where Julia, the cook, narrowly assessed her agitation. "Mr. Billy," she guessed dryly.

Tancy could not meet her eyes. Julia had raised her! She felt shamed and at fault in the presence of this lifelong authority. The cook's cynical guess made her think of Mary – pretty Mary, gone from Gaither's how long now? Months. No, years. Her baby, Jemmy, had already forgotten her. "What must I do, Julia?"

The cook shrugged and turned away. "Tain't for you to say. Just go long with what he want. He give you Mary's cabin, maybe."

"I don't want Mary's cabin!"

"And a nice little gingercake baby, long with it."

"No! I won't – I'm not old enough! Julia, help me!"

"Well, what you spect, flaunting your front parts like Mary used to? Walking around pigeon-toe, to switch your behind.

Don't think I ain't seen you."

"I never," the girl faltered.

"I *seen* you."

"If I did that, I didn't know I was doing it, honest, Julia. I have to walk some way. I can't help the way I'm built."

"It's a nice little cabin, with a store bedstead."

"I don't want any bedstead. I'd rather go on sleeping on the floor in Miss Puddin's room."

Julia rammed a chunk of wood into the firebox of the iron stove. "I've heard front door talk before, out of Mary. Same time Billy's slipping in the back door. Oh, I know the kind of fooling you're up to."

"That's a lie!"

"Girl, you calling me a liar? You watch out I don't fetch my hickory."

"You wouldn't dare," the girl challenged. "Miss Puddin said you weren't to beat me anymore. I'll tell Miss Puddin if you hit me."

"You'll tell her, huh! *I'll* tell," said Julia grimly. "She hear bout how you leading on Mr. Billy, with old Mas laying in his coffin, you wish you never had nothing worsen my hickory laid on you."

"Oh, you wouldn't tell her that, Julia? You know it isn't true!" Tancy took hold of Julia's arm. "Please say you won't tell Miss Puddin, I'll do anything you want me to — I'll give you my striped ribbon, I'll give you both my pennies. Julia, please! Somebody's got to help me!"

"Slept on straw all my life," Julia snarled. "But a nice bedstead ain't good enough for you."

There would come no help from Julia, Tancy realized. Still she timidly brought in the striped ribbon and the two pennies. Julia accepted them with a sniff, as if these gifts could not possibly be enough to assuage her resentment, her jealousy.

*

They buried Mas Gaither in the family graveyard on the north side of the orchard, between his parents, in the rank above his first wife, Nancy, and the three boys who had not survived their infancy. WILLIAM SHUFORD GAITHER read the babies' common tombstone: their mother, Nancy, had been a Shuford, cousin to Colonel Thad Shuford on the neighboring plantation.

"Nancy was too good for this world," Colonel Shuford's widow sometimes said, out of pure malice, Miss Puddin believed. No one exceeded Puddin Gaither in goodness: She read her Bible every afternoon; and delicate though she knew her nature to be, was it not Puddin who had given Gaither's Mill its heir, the incomparable Billy?

Tancy, standing behind Widow Shuford at the funeral, did not join the hymn that the preacher lined out for the mourners. Only she, of all the Gaither slaves, had been privileged to attend the burial, and she knew not to overstep.

"Will Gaither was my friend," Preacher Tomlin boomed. "My good friend and neighbor. I knew him upwards of sixty years. He was a North Carolina native, born right here in Fourth Creek community, took up where his daddy left off at the mill. Square in all his business dealings. A true patriot of these Confederate States. In sixty-one, when the war begun, Will Gaither was the first man from hereabouts to volunteer. They wouldn't take him, said he'd done his share and more in the militia. 'Well,' says Will, 'since you won't have me, you'll get two in my place,' and he give em two of his best hands to go and fight for him. That was the kind of a man Will was."

In front of Tancy, Elvira Shuford shifted. She knew, as Tancy did, that Mas Gaither's patriotism had not been entirely selfless. He was too old for duty even at the beginning of the war between the states; and as for the slaves he substituted, the master made it clear that they served for Billy, to save the boy from conscription.

"There wasn't nobody in Fourth Creek ever put their mouth out against Will Gaither," said the preacher. "No call to, he was

4

that good of a neighbor. Need a new barn? Will'd lend his crew to help you get it up, and bring the fixins for the dinner after, besides. You like to fish his creek? Hunt his woods? 'Any time, any time'; I heard him say it often; and Will would fetch his gun or his fishing stick and go with you, too. Openhanded with his corncrib, Will was, if ever you run short. Hams at butchering time. Plenty grub and welcome, if you happen onto Gaither's Mill long about dinnertime."

Miss Puddin bent her head behind her fan, overcome by the eulogy.

Her movement reminded the preacher. "Will was a *devoted husband*," he emphasized. "A devoted husband and a loving father."

Billy put his arm around his mother. At least Miss Puddin still had Billy.

"Let us pray for the soul of our departed loved one," said Preacher Tomlin.

Through the bare branches of the orchard Tancy could look upon the mossy roofs of the slave quarters, clustered in the damp hollow below the hill where the Gaither house stood. She could see the throng outside Old Swamp's cabin, gathered in deference to the hour, for Will Gaither had been a respected master. The crowd stood motionless, except for a child who cavorted in front of Mary's cabin, vacant now, with its stick-and-mud chimney in ruins. The child raced along Mary's fence to ratchet a stick against its palings. That was Jemmy — noisy, undisciplined. Mary's child.

Three years ago, when Billy was seventeen, they had hustled him into the university at mid-semester. Billy was so clever, Miss Puddin said, he would quickly catch up with his classmates.

Right after Billy left, early one morning, a slave speculator drove up in a shortbed wagon to work out a deal with Mr. Gaither. When he drove off, he carried with him Mary, screaming and wrenching at the ropes that bound her and frantically calling to Jemmy, who stood open-mouthed in the lane.

Such a thing had never happened before at Gaither's Mill, in Tancy's recollection. His slaves were like family, Mr. Gaither often said; he believed in keeping his family together.

"Let Mary be a lesson to you," Miss Puddin warned her maid.

"Yes ma'am," said Tancy, confused, but cowed. What a dumb chap she had been then! But how could she be expected to know why Mary was sold away from Gaither's? In the big house, nobody mentioned such things in her presence.

Miss Puddin said, as though explaining something, "There's no teaching morals to girls like Mary; they can't seem to learn, any more than a dog in season can."

"No ma'am," said Tancy.

"It was unfair to my Billy, keeping her on the place, and him at the most impressionable age."

"Yes ma'am."

Behind her docile responses, Tancy's emotions raged. She put on a cheerful face, but she felt like weeping at the strangest times – once when Miss Puddin hugged her unexpectedly and said for no apparent reason, "You're my good girl, Tancy."

She knew she wasn't good. Her body felt all wrong somehow, and lumpy. She was growing in the most embarrassing places, and her clothes were too tight. She looked awkward and ugly to herself in Miss Puddin's mirror; there seemed to be nothing good about her. Worse, she had started dreaming nasty. Dreams she couldn't tell about, even if there had been anyone for her to tell them to. . . .

Tancy turned her bowed head a fraction and saw Billy's eyes upon her. She felt suddenly sweaty and breathless. "Just go long with what he want," Julia had told her. What had happened to Mary could happen to Tancy, and Julia wouldn't defend her. Julia, who claimed to be like a mother to Tancy.

But Billy would be returning to school soon, Tancy told herself. Miss Puddin would see to that. The Confederate army would gobble him up if he left the university, so he had no choice, even though he wasn't much of a scholar. He had to go back to Chapel Hill. He just had to.

"Amen," said Preacher Tomlin.

"Amen," Tancy whispered.

*

In Chapel Hill, by Christmas of 1864, conscription had skimmed off all but North Carolina's youngest boys. Billy, twenty years old and sound of body, had felt uncomfortable on the campus ever since Antietam, as young veterans minus arms and legs and eyes began drifting back to classes. Their contempt of a slacker persuaded Billy, long before the holidays, and definitely after his father's death, that he was educated enough. His mother needed a man to take charge, he now insisted.

Miss Puddin thought the matter over and yielded. The war was drawing to a close, everybody said, and conscription at this point was unlikely. She retired old Swamp and designated Billy overseer in his place. She was lonely and glad to have her son at home. It was time Billy learned to run the place, she said, since he would be heir to Gaither's Mill; and every morning she called him into the library to discuss with her the mill's business and the management of their slaves.

In actual practice it was Stud who took over Swamp's job of supervising the mill gang. To Billy fell the task of doling out the weekly rations to the slaves, with his mother monitoring every cut of sowbelly, every measure of meal. He had also to write out the weekend passes, most of which Miss Puddin rescinded before they took effect.

"But if they've done their work right, why can't they go where they want?" Billy argued, during one of their early sessions.

"Dear, you can't let them do that, You'll spoil them. You mustn't treat a slave the way you would a regular hired man."

His mother selected three of the passes Billy had written out, folded them, and inserted them one at a time through the slotted grill of the library's Franklin stove. Three pretty bursts of flame made her smile. "A smart driver never spoils his slaves," she chirped.

Billy thought glumly of his university days. So what if his classmates there were cripples and his professors all senile. At least they were men who upheld a man's prerogatives. And the girls! How he missed the twittering town girls of Chapel Hill, their admiration, their respect for a university man. He desperately missed a certain accommodating barmaid in one of the hamlet's taverns. Here at Gaither's Mill Billy was just his mother's little boy, her overseer in name only, a less-than-smart slave driver.

"Suppose I don't aim to make a smart driver," he tested his mother.

"Ah, you'll learn," said she tolerantly.

"I'll not. I vow I'll turn them all loose instead. It's coming anyway, you know. It's already recorded."

"*What's* recorded? Whatever are you talking about?"

He grinned at her mockingly. "Emancipation. Surely you remember. The president of the United States, ma'am, President Lincoln, has proclaimed — "

"Hush that talk! How dare you? Jefferson Davis is our president, and I'll thank you to keep it in mind." She whirled in a fury on Tancy, who was stalking in the hall. "I see you out there, girl! Stretching your ears for what's none of your concern. Go to the kitchen and don't come back until I ring for you."

Tancy retreated down the hall, but not to the outside kitchen. Instead she swung open the door to the walkway that led there and allowed it to click audibly shut. Then she crept soundlessly under the hall stairs to "stretch her ears" for whatever she could learn. In many another such cranny, over the years, Tancy had indulged her appetite for the secrets of the house.

"You haven't given a thought to the money involved," the mother reproved her son. "When LeRoy died last year, that lost us a pretty sum, same as burying nine hundred and fifty dollars.

Worse! You can dig up buried money, but you don't dig up a dead slave. Turn the slaves loose and they're good as dead to you. Then what do you reckon happens to your profit?"

"I simply can't bear to reckon," Billy drawled.

"You'd better, my lad. Your father always worked up slave inventory at New Year's. Now here it is, past time to report our holdings, and you haven't even made a start."

"I don't know how," said Billy.

"Can't you figure out how? Your father did, and he never went to university."

"They don't teach things like this at university, and Daddy never showed me. You're the one that wants it written down. Why don't you do it?"

"All that close reading and writing?" Miss Puddin sounded horrified.

"Maybe you need specs, Mother."

"Nonsense," the woman snapped. "My eyes are as good as they ever were."

"Are you sure? Tancy reads everything to you, I notice. Here, try Daddy's old specs. If they work, you can fix up the books any way you want them."

"I do *not* need glasses," said the mother. "However, I daresay I can keep books. Mrs. Shuford does. She keeps records and writes all the drafts at their place, and takes pride in it. Myself, I had always thought it an unfeminine sort of thing to do; and you can be sure your father never would have urged me to such mannish labor." Her voice broke.

"Nor do I urge it!" Billy declared in panic. "I was only joking, Mother. I'll do it, I'll keep the books, of course." Still, after a moment he added stubbornly, "Even though it doesn't make any sense."

"You're right, honey. It doesn't make sense. But you have to keep accounts because of the infernal taxes. If you don't, they tax you so much you hardly have anything left."

So Billy brought Mas Gaither's ledgers out of the strongbox, dumped them on the library table, and began keeping the accounts. A fine mess he made of it, too, in Tancy's opinion, though she judged his work mostly by his dreadful handwriting. Tancy could write as elegant a hand as her mistress. For years she had written Miss Puddin's letters for her, and no one could have distinguished between the Spencerian flourishes of mistress and maid. Now that Billy was home, there were few letters for her to write and, alas, fewer to read, what with the erratic postal service in the winding down of war.

The war had been a dreadful inconvenience to Miss Puddin, and to most people living in the North Carolina piedmont. They had not wanted to withdraw from the Union in the first place, and they resented the Confederate powers that drafted their sons and husbands and fathers and left women to cope shorthanded with farms and businesses.

The piedmont had been spared the battles, but like the rest of the South, it suffered the grinding shortages of war. Now it seemed that the tiresome mess was about over. Miss Puddin said she would be glad when they all came to their senses and she could have real coffee to drink again and read her newspaper once more.

Since New Year's both the *Carolina Watchman* and the *Knoxford Express* had suspended publication for lack of paper. All through January the Gaithers had felt isolated from the conflict. She didn't care, Miss Puddin said; let them just shoot until they all killed each other off or one side got tired and quit; and it didn't matter to her which side that was.

Tancy missed the newspaper more than her mistress did. For years she had read every piece of written matter that came into the house at Gaither's Mill. Whenever her mistress napped, she snooped through the letters and papers on the library table. Emancipation? She could probably tell more about it than Billy could; but to whom? She wasn't like the other slaves at Gaither's, with family and friends to talk to, and certainly she couldn't discuss anything with Julia or Miss Puddin. Still she read compulsively whatever she could get her hands on, for she was tantalized by the forbidden, avid for some knowledge she could not put a name to.

Soon after Billy took Mas Gaither's ledgers from the strongbox and left them on the library table, Tancy began her secret examination of the plantation's records, for want of anything better to read. Before February was out, in Mas Gaither's daybook for the year 1848, the year Tancy was born, she came across a baffling, illuminating entry:

> 6/16/48 – Lulu lying in.
> 6/17/48 – Lulu delivered of Tancy. Both well.

That's me! was Tancy's first thought, charmed to find her name written there; and then almost at once the meaning of her discovery filled her with guilt. Lulu lying in, Lulu delivered, 1848 . . . this Lulu had to have been her mother.

Mas Gaither's daybook answered a question that she had never felt privileged to ask. The revelation of what for years she had instinctively, unconsciously sought overwhelmed her. She wanted to run and hide. She wanted to run and tell somebody. She wanted –

I want my mother, she realized.

2

T ANCY'S INITIAL EXHILARATION gave way to misgivings. Was that Lulu truly her mother? Then what had become of her once Tancy was born? Where was she now?

"I don't know nothing about any Lulu, nothing whatsoever," Julia said, when Tancy asked. Obstinate Julia. Only when it suited her did she share her secrets, and today it did not suit. Tancy would have to plot a different approach.

Old Swamp remembered a Louella, however, sold off at the time of the bad flood when the best bottomland washed out and the marse came up short of cash. Or was the name Lucy? Lucille? Swamp shook his head. He never had studied names much.

As soon as she could, Tancy checked the ledger. The entry definitely read *Lulu*, a pet name for Louella perhaps, or Lucille. The Nancy must have been a mistake the master had corrected. But June 17, 1848 was no mistake — that was definitely Tancy's birthday! She didn't know a single other slave with a real birthday. Most of them claimed the Fourth of July or New Year's or the anniversary of somebody in the big house, for the honor of it.

Tancy, however, had been written up officially in the master's daybook. She had been taken note of.

She itched to know more. It wasn't going to be as easy as it looked, with the ledgers lying loose on the library table. Years of prying had taught her useful deceits, but a recent close call with the mistress daunted her.

"What are you doing in the library?" Mrs. Gaither had demanded.

Said Tancy, ready with her answer, "Looking for your fan, Miss Puddin."

"Are you blind? I've got it here in my hand."

"I mean your Sunday fan, Miss Puddin." Tancy shuffled the ledgers about and contrived a discovery. "Yes, here it is." She unfurled the dainty silver ribs.

"What's that doing on the library table?"

"I must have put it there," Tancy replied truthfully; then with guile, "You wanted it Sunday afternoon, remember, when you looked for the preacher to call."

"I did?" The mistress pondered, frowned, shook her head. "All right, put it back where it belongs. But hereafter, mind what you do with my valuables. I don't intend to follow around picking up after you."

"No ma'am," said Tancy.

*

Although its weatherboarding and high porches made it the finest in the community, the big house at Gaither's Mill was not really large. The snug cabin built by the first settlers on Fourth Creek sheltered four generations of canny millers before Will Gaither, to favor his sweet Puddin, added the two bedrooms that comprised the second story. The downstairs rooms subsequently became parlor, dining room, and library. With Billy and the mistress in and out of the library that winter, Tancy's search for Lulu dragged.

The Gaithers used a bona fide library table for a desk, but except for the ledgers upon it and Mrs. Gaither's Bible, their "library" housed no other books. The Franklin stove warmed the place in winter, and a cross draft cooled it in summer. Three layers of rugs cushioning the floor represented the number of times the mistress had redecorated the parlor. The library had, in fact, inherited the parlor's best mistakes — the rugs, the table, a tin oil lamp with a green glass shade, three unrelated chairs, and a mammoth chaise longue supported by eight legs and upholstered in fabric the color of mildew. In the parlor were stylish plush chairs and a matching sofa mounted on china casters, but the Gaithers used the parlor only when visitors came. The library was more comfortable.

In the library, therefore, on a Sunday afternoon late in February, after Billy had ridden off to call upon the four unmarried Shuford daughters, Mrs. Gaither lay upon the chaise longue while Tancy read aloud from the Bible. The low-riding winter sun shone benignly through the large single-paned window and reinforced the warmth of the Franklin stove. In this hothouse atmosphere Mrs. Gaither fluttered her Sunday fan.

" 'And these are the names of the children of Israel, which came into Egypt,' " Tancy droned, with an eye on the fan, " 'Jacob and his sons: Reuben, Jacob's firstborn. And the sons of Reuben: Honoch, and Phallu, and Hezron, and Carmi.' "

Before long, the fan idled.

" 'And the sons of Simeon: Jemuel and Jamin, and Ohad,' " Tancy whispered, " 'and Jachin, and Zohar, and Shaul, the son of a Canaanitish woman.' "

Miss Puddin's head drooped and gently she smacked her lips, pouting even in her sleep.

Tancy slid from her chair placed behind the chaise (Mrs. Gaither allowed no one to look upon her face while she meditated) and started to ransack the pile on the library table. A half hour or so later, while Miss Puddin dozed and muttered and dozed again,

14

a line in Mas Gaither's account book miraculously leaped to the slave girl's eye.

9/9/49 — Lulu sold to Thad Shuford $600

"Oh!" Tancy exclaimed involuntarily.

"Nyum-nyum-yum," groaned Miss Puddin.

Tancy slipped back to her chair. " 'The sons of Judah — ' "

The silver fan jerked to attention. "That's enough of those old sons," the woman ordered.

Tancy sat silent. I wasn't but a year old, she thought. *Mother!* She thought of Jemmy out there in the lane, watching while his mother was taken away.

"Read me something out of the newspaper."

"Newspaper's stopped, Miss Puddin." Tancy spoke with an effort.

"Read me one of the old ones, then. About the fellow that got caught in the steel mill and it rolled him out twelve feet long."

The girl hesitated. "It's Sunday. . . ."

"Well, you think I don't know that?" the woman snapped. "No, no, no; leave that paper lay! You know I don't read anything secular on Sunday."

She was fully awake now and would not go back to sleep. Still she grumbled drowsily on. "I dearly love Scripture, but I can't see the sense of the begats. Every one of them sons! Didn't those folks have any daughters, I wonder?" She stood up, shook out her long black skirt, and turned around for inspection. "How does my hair look in back?"

"Nice, Miss Puddin; real nice. Wait once, here's a place I must not've fixed right this morning." With deft fingers Tancy repaired the nap's damages. "You have such pretty hair, Miss Puddin. Like pure gold."

"Well," said the woman. As familiar boots sounded on the front porch, she cocked her head. "Billy?"

Billy drew aside the fringed curtain that separated parlor and library. "Finished with your nap, I see."

His mother bridled. "You know I never nap in the daytime."

"All done meditating, then."

"I thought you rode over to Shufords'?"

"Halfway there I crossed the missus coming to call here, so I rode back with her. She's out front in the carriage. I told her I'd see if you were awake."

"Billy, you know I don't nap in the daytime," his mother began, but Billy was not listening to her. His eyes were on Tancy, eyes glistening in the way she now understood. His mother understood too, and she took his arm. "We'll go out to Mrs. Shuford," she said firmly. "Did one of the girls drive with her?" She spoke across his shoulder to Tancy. "Run upstairs, girl, and get my silver fan." Her gaze commanded the girl's. *Don't come back down*, it said.

Tancy refrained from looking at the silver fan that the mistress held concealed in the folds of her skirt. Miss Puddin might be foolish, but she was no fool.

She went upstairs, but not to her mistress's room. That would be the first place Billy looked, if he gave his mother the slip. Instead, she crept into the lumber room, where a shed window sifted dusty light over old trunks and discarded schoolbooks and furniture. Into a swayback settee she sank to catch her breath and to tune her ear to the household. She had always been a good listener: she had always had to be.

The lumber room, where Tancy hid from Billy, occupied the cramped area over the front porch. A cupboard door at the end of the upstairs hall gave access to it. Sun beating on the embossed metal roof made it blistering hot on summer days, and in winter the wind whistled through generous cracks.

On this winter Sunday, however, the piedmont basked in mellow warmth, gift of a climate so reliably gracious that most

16

North Carolinians, if they gave it any thought at all, counted it their due.

The company conversation funneled upward into Tancy's hiding place, polite voices of son and daughter, the chatter of mothers.

Mother, Tancy grieved. She grieved for herself, for the motherless child; she almost wanted to cry. But crying was what Miss Puddin did to get her way. None of that for Tancy. She would simply ask Mrs. Shuford about Lulu. Have you got my mother? she would say to her. Yet the prospect of asking frightened Tancy. Slaves answered questions, relayed questions between masters, but slaves themselves never questioned.

She heard the front door open and Billy's tread on the porch. Taking the Shuford girl out to the well for a drink, she guessed. A glance out of the shed window confirmed this. Billy and Miss Pleas, christened Pleasant.

There were two wells at Gaither's Mill, one below the kitchen in back, the other for the family's exclusive use, in the front yard. Stout brush fences kept chickens and pigs out of the yard, which was bare of grass but colorful with flowers in their season, in beds outlined by whitewashed stones. Whited stones also marked the graveled paths that curved down to the gate, across to the well, and back to the house. Along this triangular promenade, Billy accompanied Pleasant Shuford.

She had better be pleasant, Tancy observed spitefully, for handsome she was not. She was as chunky in form as Billy was, and heavy-browed. Like her mother, she shot her jaw when she talked, and cords in her neck stood out. But Billy inclined his head to her and guided her over the pebbles as though assisting the daintiest of creatures. Tancy had seen him do as much for Miss Diligent Shuford, when Dilly accompanied her mother on the afternoon call, and for Miss Temperance and Miss Prudent in turn.

The truth was Billy couldn't keep his hands off young women, and nobody knew that better than Tancy. On the far side of the well, he caressed their fingertips and gently touched their waists. The sloping yard and a deeply pitched roof over the well housing concealed today's mild courtship, should the mothers be watching from the parlor window. From the shed dormer Tancy had a good view, and she studied the romancing hopefully. She wished Billy would marry one of the Shuford girls. That would certainly solve a lot of problems.

"They're clearing out the prison in Salisbury!" Mrs. Shuford shouted from below.

Tancy kept her eyes on the well while she followed the parlor conversation. Mrs. Shuford was the one who brought them word of the war, for she often drove into Salisbury on business, where a telegraph office at the railroad station posted the news. Billy, with a glance toward the house, now kissed Pleasant right on the lips. And Miss Pleas brazenly leaned against him and kissed him back!

Tancy hugged herself for joy. That just had to mean they were engaged! Miss Puddin wouldn't mind, and as for Miss Elvira — well, Colonel Thad Shuford, the father, had died at Second Manassas. To four unmarried women running a plantation — five, counting the widow Elvira — and none of them getting any younger, Billy would be a godsend.

The fortunate Miss Pleas wrapped herself in her shawl and started for the house, Billy cradling her elbow. She spoke coquettishly to him, her chin jutting as she smiled, her neck cords leaping.

This was it! They were coming inside to announce their engagement! Tancy pressed her nose to the windowpane, just as Billy glanced up at the dormer. She fell back, mortified to be caught spying.

From below, Mrs. Shuford continued to rail against what was happening in Salisbury. "Prisoners taking up every blessed place in the railroad cars!"

18

Tancy waited for the happy commotion that would follow the young couple's announcement.

"It's that fool in Richmond," the widow lamented. "Jeff Davis, taking over our railroad cars for Yankee prisoners."

"Now, Ma," said Miss Pleas. "You talk like the railroad belongs to us."

"And so it does, miss. It's got our name on it—the North Carolina Railroad; that means it belongs to this state, and Jeff Davis has got no business filling it up with Yankees."

Miss Pleas said tranquilly, "Well, you been wanting the Yankees to get out of North Carolina."

That didn't sound like any bride talking, Tancy realized with disappointment. She felt vexed, puzzled, shocked by a young woman who would kiss a man like that and then march in the house and boldly start arguing politics. Tancy simply didn't understand love, she saw that now. Perhaps even Miss Puddin didn't know all the rules.

They continued talking politics downstairs. Tancy could tell by Miss Puddin's indifferent murmur. Elvira Shuford knew every last thing about the Petersburg siege, and she told every last thing too; she rambled on about generals on both sides, Early and Pickett and Johnston and Sherman. Boring.

Still, Miss Puddin welcomed her neighbor's visits, for Elvira sometimes brought with her a nice little packet of tea, of all things, and tea had been as scarce as salt in the county for more than two years. Growing up in the back country, Elvira had schooled in all there was to know about bartering. Her mules got shod, her corn got ground, she found salt in Salisbury months after every grain in the town had supposedly vanished. Furthermore, she and her daughters had ridden the railroad cars on a pass, not once, but several times, between Salisbury and Statesville, twenty-five miles away.

"And quick as they get the prison cleared out," she promised Mrs. Gaither, "me and you'll take ourselves a ride on the cars, we will."

Oh no, Miss Puddin protested, not for her such bold adventures. Twenty-five miles!

"Sure you can." Now Elvira bawled from the front door, where she stood stretching out her departure. "What you want to do is take your gal along, that's how the town ladies do it, take their maid with them on the train and go around to all the shops or visiting, or whatever they want to do, until it's time to get on the cars and go back home. Do it in a day and eat your supper at home."

Tancy thrilled. Mrs. Shuford said it so casually — "Take your gal along." Adventure!

Tancy had never seen a railroad train, but she knew what one looked like from newspaper pictures; and she knew about adventure from a wonderful book that belonged to Billy, about a boy named Rollo and his father, who traveled on a steamship and a stagecoach and maybe a railroad train too, that carried them all over the world.

Mas Gaither had driven his wife and young son into Statesville to watch the first cars arrive on the new tracks laid for the western extension of the North Carolina Railroad. The sight had thoroughly dismayed Miss Puddin. The engine was dirty and noisy and frightening, and she had no wish to see the thing again, or any other like it, and she hoped she never had to ride any machine that ground forward on a pair of insignificant metal rails — it just had to be dangerous.

But, Elvira insisted, the trains had been running for years now without accident, and the way they looked outside wasn't a clue to how nice they looked inside; just beautiful! And comfortable . . . well, like sitting in your own parlor! And fast! You had to ride before you'd believe anything could go that fast.

Her animated voice diminished as the party drifted down the porch steps toward the gate.

Tancy lay back on the settee, ecstatic at the thought of riding in a railroad car. She had never ridden in a buggy even; and now it might happen, thanks to Mrs. Elvira Shuford, that she would get to ride in the fastest vehicle that ever traveled on wheels! Would she be scared? Did the train go so fast it made you dizzy? If she got sick, like that time on the grapevine swing – but she decided not to think about that. She would wash and iron her white apron the day before the trip, and her white bandanna, and she could blacken her shoes and carry a basket for the articles Miss Puddin would buy in the shops –

"Little Tancy! Are you waiting for me, Tancy?" Suddenly there was Billy towering over her, his ruddy cheeks huge in her dilated vision, his lips wetly gleaming.

Tancy, engrossed in her fantasy of riding on the train, had not heard him enter the lumber room – she, who always listened! In a panic, she started up, but Billy expertly rolled over the back of the settee and landed on top of her, forcing the breath from her lungs and effectively pinning her down.

"Oh, Billy!" she gasped.

"Sh-h-h. Don't talk," he whispered. He began panting and pulling at her clothes.

She locked her arms over her chest. He jerked at her wrists. "Come on, Tancy," he entreated. "Be nice to me."

Nice? She wanted to scream for help, it was all she could do to keep herself from screaming. But whom could she call? Billy was the master, and she was only a slave; it wasn't for her to decide. Just go along, Julia had instructed her. She froze with terror underneath his frantic body.

"Open, Tancy – " In haste, he fumbled up her skirts. She clamped her knees together. His fingers yanked at the drawstrings of her undergarment. He forced her legs apart. He whimpered like a hurt animal, but there was nothing hurt about him, he was strong, his fingers –

"No!" Her shriek ended abruptly as he stopped up her mouth. She moaned despairingly. No other's hands had ever touched her in that place, she was on fire, she was suffocating! "Oh Lord, oh Lord, help me, Lord!" she prayed, but his palm muffled her prayer, and anyway, she knew the Lord wasn't listening.

"Open," Billy pleaded, clawing between her legs.

In a surge of new strength, she twisted and thrashed beneath his heavy body.

"Ahhh!" Billy sighed, and collapsed upon her as the lumber room door opened and Miss Puddin said sternly, "Billy. Tancy. What do you think you're doing in here?"

3

"GO AWAY, MOTHER," Billy mumbled.

"What do you mean, 'Go away'? This is *my* house!"

"I'm sorry, Mother. Please, Mother—" He squirmed off the settee and on his knees, back to her, adjusted his trousers.

Tancy leaped up and scurried for the door where Miss Puddin waited with her fan. A blow across her forehead stunned her. She stumbled across the sill and warded off a second blow with upraised hand—a mistake, for the fan caught her little finger with a peculiar crack.

"Oh!" she gasped. She tried to run, but her loosened drawers dropped to her ankles and hobbled her. She fell to the floor and scrabbled toward the stairway.

"Shame, you little hussy!" her mistress spat after her; and "Shame!" she spat at her son. "Your *own sister!*" She closed herself inside the lumber room with him.

Alone on the landing, Tancy fastened up her drawers in a daze. Her mind worked sluggishly. Sister. Shame. Billy's own sister.

She felt no shame; she felt no pain. Her little finger crooked jauntily, and she inspected it with odd calm, as though looking at some foreign object. The knuckle appeared to be thickening, but it was not the first time she had received swollen knuckles from Miss Puddin.

Her clothing hampered her body. She smoothed her skirts as slowly she descended the stairs, endeavoring to shake free her petticoat wadded underneath. By the time she reached the kitchen, she had begun shivering and whispering to herself. Shame. Shame. She ran behind the woodbox and crouched there, nursing her finger.

Julia surveyed her with slitted eyes. "Billy again. Let's see." She reached for the girl's wrist.

"Go away!" Tancy screamed. "Don't touch me!"

Julia slapped her face smartly. "Hush that. You ain't the boss here." She did, however, refrain from touching her hand, and instead began poking through her medical stores. Number 2 liniment no longer stocked her box. Months ago, together with all the local doctors, it had gone to war. Julia's herbs and remedies were better than any doctor's, she insisted, but she did miss Number 2.

She fished a short section of bamboo from her box and split it with a butcher knife. Then she studied Tancy's hand. "That little'un been broke," she announced, and she would have begun treating the finger, but the girl shook so violently that Julia had to reprimand her. "Get ahold of yourself, girl."

"I'm cold." Tancy's teeth chattered, and her head jerked.

The cook brought the quilt she kept in the pantry for muffling yeast doughs and threw it across the girl's shoulders. "Now hold still." She plastered the afflicted finger with grease, feathers, and nettle leaves, and bound it inside the bamboo splint with a yucca string. Tancy made no outcry, but tears slid unceasingly down her face.

"There," said Julia with satisfaction; and then irritably, "Crying.

What you gonna do when it really starts hurting? And it gonna hurt, I garntee, whole lot worsen it do now."

Tancy huddled, wretched, under the quilt. "I'm all wet."

"My land, girl, if you wasn't more growed than to wet your draws! Don't just set there, go clean yourself up." But the girl still shook, and the woman relented. "All right, give me your draws and I'll throw them out in the washtub. But I ain't washing them for you, hear? Girl as growed as you are has to wash her own, if she can't hold her water."

Tancy disrobed in the modesty of her quilt. "My underskirt too – " she whispered.

Julia examined the garments. She swiveled her eyes toward the big house. "That ain't no pee," she declared. "That there's spunky, a man's spunk, don't try to tell me any different." She shook out the clothes and found a smear of blood. "Aha!" she cried.

At the sight of blood, Tancy collapsed. "I'm bleeding!" she wept. "Help me, Julia! Am I going to die?"

Julia snorted. "Ain't nobody never died from that, not that I knowed of."

"It hurts me so. He tore my, down there, tore my – "

"Your nature," the cook said swiftly. To Julia, no sexual part was so vile as its true name.

"I was up in the lumber room, hiding, and he caught me. I was so scared I didn't know what to do – "

Caustically, "So he did it for you."

"No, he never!"

"How come you bleeding then?"

"I didn't say he did that with his . . . his – "

"Nature," Julia supplied automatically. Then, in surprise, "He never?"

"No. Not with his nature. I don't know what happened, it all went so fast."

Julia snickered. "There's many a cooter too fast for the rabbit."

"What does that mean?" Tancy inquired timidly.

The cook soaked a rag with warm water from the stove reservoir. "There. Wash and dry yourself good. If you wipe on some of this grease, that'll help too." Her tone was unexpectedly mild, but when she stumped out of the kitchen, she cackled vindictively, "Yessir, many a cooter, hee-hee-hee!"

Julia was the prestigious doctor-cook at Gaither's Mill. Her herbs and charms cured earache and sore gums. She could lessen the pains of menstruation and childbirth; she knew how to make measles erupt. Her lore had passed to her from her grandmother, who claimed to be an African princess; Aheenti could show you six ring marks of her country around her neck to prove it, Old Swamp remembered, and in her earlobes, holes you could stick a chicken bone through.

In Julia the ghost of Aheenti still walked, Swamp said; and indeed, the cook's measured pace was that of royalty. Across her nose and cheeks she wore the regal tattoos of her grandmother. Her neck was long and her eyes had the lidless look of a snake's. She saw everything, Tancy had always believed; she knew secrets.

Tancy's finger was throbbing by the time Julia returned. The woman had, after all, washed the underclothes, and now she spread the wet garments on a rack before the fireplace. "You warmed up any?" she asked.

"Some." Tancy felt comforted, in spite of her finger, just by Julia's asking.

Julia said, "How you going to splain a broke finger to the mistis?"

"Miss Puddin was the one who broke it," said Tancy. "I shouldn't have to explain that."

"She was there? When it happened? In the lumber room?"

The cook's greedy questioning alerted Tancy. She said, watching Julia, "Miss Puddin told Billy, 'Shame on you, Billy Gaither, Tancy is your *own sister!*'"

Julia expelled a breath. "She say!"

In the fireplace, a cinder exploded upward and dropped with a *zsh* into Julia's cooking pot. Tancy waited.

But Julia turned away. She set her medicine box back on the shelf. She uncovered the flour barrel and measured handfuls into her bread bowl.

Tell me your secrets, Tancy begged silently. *Tell me who I am.* In a small voice she said, "I didn't know I was Billy's sister."

"You ain't. No such thing as brother and sister between white folks and black. You and Billy got the same daddy, is all." Julia began squeezing yeast sponge into her flour.

It was true, then. My daddy, Tancy thought in wonderment. Mas Gaither was my daddy. "Have I got any real brothers or sisters?"

"Sure. Alexander and Go-Charlie. They gone for good now. Don't tell me you've forgot your own brothers." But Julia blinked, thinking back. "No, you wouldn't remember, cause you was still a sucking baby when Mas sold Lucy off, and that was how come those chaps run off, before they was growed, hardly."

"When Mas sold Lucy off — ?" Tancy prompted.

"He had to," Julia said. "He might of knowed the mistis would find out about Lucy."

Who wouldn't mark a woman that lived in a cabin to herself? Julia demanded. Excused from evening tasks, allowed to lay out sick without punishment, not to mention the times Mas Gaither would go to her cabin in the afternoons.

"But he paid for it," said the cook. "Miss Puddin never let him forget." It was Miss Puddin who took the baby Tancy into the big house, to be a constant reproach to the master. They had some words about that, and it took Miss Puddin a while, but she finally broke him down. Julia punched her dough with powerful, angry blows.

"Lucy . . ." Tancy tried the name on her tongue. "Lucy — that was my mother's name?"

Julia grunted.

"What was she like?"

"I don't remember," Julia said shortly. "Don't matter, noways. No telling where she's ended up."

Tancy dared not press her further. Julia had already told her enough to fill her heart with joy. She belonged to a real family. Alexander and Go-Charlie might be gone for good, but they had been real brothers; and she understood now why she had always loved Mas Gaither. He was her daddy!

He had been kind to her in special ways, she realized – gave her that striped ribbon for Christmas; and more than once, after a trip to Statesville, he slipped her a piece of candy from the packets he brought back for Billy.

As for her mother, Tancy knew a secret that Julia didn't. She knew where to start asking for Lucy, just as soon as she could work up the nerve to ask.

"Feel if them draws ain't dry yet," Julia said. "I want that quilt back to rise my bread."

*

Miss Puddin regretted Tancy's broken finger and said so. "But it was your own fault for sticking your hand out," she argued. However, she did examine her fan pensively; its silver ribs were charmingly worked to resemble a peacock's spread tail. She must have seen that it became a weapon when folded though, for when she undressed for bed that night, she did not scold about the extra time it took her maid to unlace her corsets; and she herself helped remove her golden tortoiseshell hairpins.

"I suppose my hair will look a mess until you get that stupid splint off your finger," she remarked.

"No ma'am," said Tancy loyally. "I don't use that finger much, anyway."

"Be just my luck, to have to go around with my hair hanging down in strings, like Elvira Shuford's."

28

"No, Miss Puddin. Mrs. Shuford's hair is ratty, like nobody ever brushes it for her. Yours is all soft and shiny, like a girl's."

"Well," said Mrs. Gaither.

Julia was right about Tancy's finger hurting worse. Pain made her feverish that night, and it was all she could do to stifle her sighs. She twisted on her pallet, fearful of waking her mistress.

But long after the candle had been snuffed, when Tancy supposed that she alone watched out the night, Mrs. Gaither spoke from her bed in a kindly voice. "You understand, Tancy, that God punishes girls who let young men make free with their private parts."

The girl winced.

Sternly, Mrs. Gaither went on: "You mustn't pretend that you don't understand what I'm saying to you. Today. In the lumber room. Mr. Billy."

"But I didn't do anything! I didn't, Miss Puddin. I begged him not to, but he – "

"I don't want to hear any of that, Tancy. You surely know what young men are like. They can't help themselves; it's their nature. It is your duty not to let such things happen, for it is a sin, and God will surely punish you for it."

Mrs. Gaither's punishment might precede God's, she threatened. For a girl like Tancy, living closely within the family and daily inviting a vulnerable young man to temptation, it was necessary for Miss Puddin to speak plainly to her, like a mother. That was what mothers were for.

On and on she droned, until at last she droned herself asleep.

Alone once more with her pain, Tancy blew gently upon her finger. It burned like fire – that would be the nettles. She was conscious too of her aching crotch, and imagined naively that this was God's punishment for what Billy had done to her. Miss Puddin's punishment she accepted stoically – that was a mistress's privilege – but the mother part confused her. Was a mother truly just another punisher? Weren't God and Miss Puddin enough?

For the first time in her conscious years, she felt a stirring of disloyalty. No matter how Miss Puddin expressed it, she was *not* Tancy's mother. Lucy was; Lucy, who resided as Lulu in Mas Gaither's ledger, real, taken note of.

A real mother, Tancy dreamed, *my* real mother would not punish me for what somebody else did.

4

TANCY HAD ALWAYS delighted in dressing Mrs. Gaither's hair. The broken finger, however, so hampered her that the customary hour for hairdressing lengthened into two, and on shampoo days, lasted well through the morning. And now, many another leisurely task united mistress and maid in a tactic which neither mentioned: keeping Tancy out of Billy's way.

"That finger of yours is a nuisance," the mistress complained falsely. "Right when Billy needs me most."

Tancy said, "Yes'm," and lifted a lock of hair to examine the roots.

Mrs. Gaither said, "Is it looking dull? I'd better dry it in the sun today."

"With maybe some of Julia's rinse," Tancy suggested. The word *bleach* was never spoken between them.

When her mistress wasn't looking, Tancy flirted with her reflection in the mirror. Miss Puddin said vanity was a sin, so she reminded those velvety, mocking eyes that decent girls used the mirror only to make sure they looked decent. How was it that a mirror never took you seriously?

As for Billy, he gladly dropped the library sessions with his mother and spent his days at the mill. Learning the business from the ground up, he informed his mother, when he appeared at the house for meals; and since he made heavy work of keeping books on Stud's labor down at the mill, she did not protest.

The ragged stone foundation of Gaither's Mill rose against the high bluff of a rocky branch off Fourth Creek, which for a few miles southward paralleled the Charlotte road. The first Gaither had had the foresight to install French buhrs for grinding wheat, and by the time his descendant, Will, took over, the business had become a full-fledged merchant mill, buying wheat and selling flour. Wartime had curtailed mill profits, and the shortage of tools and laborers reduced Gaither's worked land by half, but it was the same all over — everybody's fences needed repairs; everybody made do with plows mended for the fourth and fifth times; nobody had enough help to run a plantation properly. Still the mill wheel turned, grinding corn on the snares now, for customers who could not pay cash.

Gaither's was more than a mill — it was a gathering place for the community's farmers, a place for politicking and gossip. To Billy, still hankering after the maidens of Chapel Hill, it became a refuge from his mother. If he no longer enjoyed the conquests of his college days, he could at least do his share of boasting about them with other men, down at the mill.

From time to time, that February of 1865, a few Confederate soldiers stopped in, bringing news of the war and tales of ravishment that incensed the mill regulars — and especially Billy. Slaughter, pillage, rape, all through the South! While Billy tamely minded the mill.

"They say the whole city of Columbia's been burnt to the ground!" he reported at the dining room table.

"Serves them right," Mrs. Gaither sniffed. "It was South Carolina that dragged the rest of us into the old war. North Carolina never was for it."

"Well, the fellows claim it's about over."

Tancy, at her station behind the mistress's chair, listened avidly.

Mrs. Gaither said, "They told the same last year, when Atlanta fell. I'll believe it when they send all the boys home."

"Some of these boys aren't waiting to be sent," Billy said. The Confederate soldiers out on the road these days were deserters, and not ashamed to admit it. They still wore their army jackets and caps. There were crowds of them over Raleigh way, Billy had heard, and not enough jails to hold the ones that got caught.

"They're probably going home to do the spring plowing," said Mrs. Gaither. "I don't blame them one bit."

"You'll blame them when the Yankees come and turn your niggers loose."

"Go to the kitchen, Tancy," said Mrs. Gaither sharply. "Tell Tish I'll have my pudding now."

"Can't you ring the bell for it, Mother?" Billy taunted.

"Git, girl. Do what I say. Go on out to the kitchen."

Tancy left the room, but loitered in the hallway to listen.

"Don't talk like that in front of Tancy," the mother scolded her son. "One of these days she'll get to thinking she can just cut out of here, if she feels like it."

"That's what the war is about," Billy reminded her.

"But Tancy doesn't know that."

Yes, I do! Tancy thought, with mingled fear and elation. She rushed to the kitchen and demanded pudding in a tone that made Tish, the serving girl, gape.

In the dining room, Mrs. Gaither reversed her argument smoothly. This wasn't such a bad war, she said, with an air of pardoning the conflict. Inconveniences, deprivations — even going without her tea and sugar and the newspaper — these were small burdens to bear for all the North Carolina piedmont had been spared. Its towns had not been burned, its houses had not been ransacked, its women (she pointed out piously) had not been insulted.

Insulted – ! Billy ground his teeth and left the table.

*

As if to even things out, in March of 1865 war crossed the Tennessee border and ripped through the peaceful North Carolina piedmont. Like a spring tornado, the Union general George Stoneman's cavalry stormed through the western part of the state, striking without warning at remote hamlets in the Smokies. The general raided Boone one day, raced along the Yadkin River the next, flattened Wilkesboro.

"Billy says he's coming down the Charlotte road," Mrs. Gaither wailed to Elvira Shuford. Every day the two women met to exchange rumors of Stoneman's latest strategy. "You know, he's headed for Statesville; he'll destroy us!"

The pragmatic Elvira said, "Ain't nothing here or in Statesville to draw him. There is in Salisbury. He'll turn loose the Yankee soldiers they got penned up in the old cotton factory there, is my guess."

"Yankee soldiers! In Salisbury?"

"They been there all along," said Elvira. "Ten thousand of them in prison there. Been shipping them out on the railroad cars ever since Christmas. I told you all that before."

When Elvira left, Mrs. Gaither paced the floor. "Turned them loose!" she exclaimed to Tancy. "Ten thousand Yankee soldiers, turned loose to prey on innocent women!"

Tancy was frightened. How was she to defend Miss Puddin against any Yankee, let alone ten thousand?

Billy said Yankees had stripped naked a Lenoir woman who had sewed gold pieces into her corset.

"Oh, my spoons, my silver wedding spoons," Mrs. Gaither moaned. "Tancy, go fetch my spoons. We'll bury them in the garden."

"That's the first place they look," said Billy.

"My jewelry — I can't let them take my wedding ring. And my mourning brooch! What am I to do?"

"You could hide it in your hair, Miss Puddin," Tancy suggested, inspired. "We'll put your ring and things underneath your knot, in back, and I'll pin your hair over them good — "

"Nonsense! What if the Yankees suspected? You heard what they did to that Lenoir woman." The mistress looked at Tancy thoughtfully. "I suppose we could sew the silver under your clothes somewhere."

"Better do something with it," Billy advised. He felt cheated of any role in the drama taking place, and in his envious state, magnified the propaganda that came to him. He relayed stories of feather pillows torn apart and floorboards ripped up, he told of sick babies turned out of their cradles under suspicion of harboring treasure in their mattresses. The alarm he raised in his mother amused him.

So Tancy strung the wedding spoons along a cord passed around her waist and trained herself to a gait that prevented any telltale jingle.

Stoneman's raiders departed from Wilkesboro, not south to Statesville or Salisbury, but north, through Mount Airy into Virginia. God's salvation, Mrs. Gaither said, so thankful of reprieve that she overlooked the enemy in her own front yard. Nearly every day, men traveling north on the Charlotte road came through her gate for a drink at the well. Not all wore uniforms, and until a civil fellow wearing the Union blue rapped at the door and offered to buy a guinea hen, she had assumed the men were Confederates.

"Indeed, I'll not trade with a Yankee," she informed the man.

"Then I'll save my money and my manners," he retorted cheerfully. He was out the gate before she noticed that he carried the guinea under his jacket.

That was only the beginning. It was also the only offer of

payment she ever got. In pairs the men came as well as singly, and more and more in groups. Sometimes they asked for food; mostly they took what they found, Rebels and Yankees alike. One crowd rooted up all the turnips that had wintered over in the garden, and Mrs. Gaither rejoiced that she had not buried the silver there; but then the ragtag mob cornered six chickens from her flock and roasted them right in her own yard.

"What kind of upbringing did those Yankees have?" she demanded of Billy.

"Those aren't Yankees, Ma; they're bushwhackers."

"What's *bushwhackers,* for mercy's sake?"

"Irregulars. Hoodlums, roaming around, stealing and so forth. They're a bad problem north of here, they say. Got a regular fort up by Wilkesboro, with guns and a stockade and everything."

The fort was manned by Rebel deserters and escaped conscripts banding together, Billy said. They lived off the countryside, stealing what they needed for their guerrilla operation.

Mrs. Gaither said, "Well, I guess I don't begrudge a few chickens to boys that are just trying to stay out of the army." She smiled fondly on her own boy, who had also evaded service.

"Would you begrudge a few horses?" Billy asked. "Or cows?" Any time the bushwhackers ran across a horse they liked better than their own, they took it. And Billy heard for a fact that they would chop the steak part out of a steer for their dinner, and leave the rest of the carcass to rot.

"Oh, my soul!" said Mrs. Gaither. She rang the alarm signal on the plantation bell. When the women and children came in response, she sent them to pen the cattle in the farthest pasture. She ordered Billy and Stud to drive the horses and mules to a corral deep in the woods beyond the slave quarters. While they were gone, she received an ominous visitor.

"Captain Coite Murdock, ma'am, of Branch's Brigade," the Confederate officer introduced himself. "Here in reference to one William Gaither of this plantation."

Mrs. Gaither clutched Tancy's arm for support. "You will have to look for him in Chapel Hill," she said, in a high, unnatural voice. "My son is a student there."

"And for the conscription of same, when apprehended," the man continued.

"President Swain has arranged for young boys in the university to be exempted."

"That's boys under eighteen, ma'am. Your son is twenty, I understand."

"If you understand that, you are mistaken."

"In fact, he is no longer a student. Your son must be aware, if you are not, that he became eligible for duty when he left the university."

Four men trotted around the corner of the house, laughing and driving a squealing young pig before them. They wore gray Confederate forage caps and carried rifles slung across their shoulders.

"Attention!" shouted Captain Murdock.

The men wheeled and raced for the woods. The pig ran under the porch.

"Stop them!" cried Mrs. Gaither. "They're stealing my pig."

"Your pig is safe, ma'am."

"But *I'm* not! After them! You've got a pistol — use it!"

The captain coughed into his fist. "There's four of them," he mentioned, "and only one of me."

"What on earth are you saying? Standing there watching those men rob me! I'm being robbed constantly, *constantly*. If it isn't the Yankees, it's the bushwhackers, and if it isn't the bushwhackers, it's the deserters."

"I agree it is a problem, ma'am."

"You agree *what* is a problem?"

"This, this, this deserter problem we seem to be having, general disorganization, and so forth."

"Well, who's responsible for that, I'd like to know? Here you are, a *licensed* officer, hunting down my poor little boy like an animal, and you let four great brutes go free."

The captain looked abashed. "I'm sorry."

"Sorry . . . !" Mrs. Gaither bowed her head behind her fan. "I am a widow, sir, a helpless woman. Why a gentleman of your rank should so punish a helpless widow, I cannot think — " She broke into sobs.

The officer did not wait for her to complete her thoughts about a gentleman of his rank. He untied the horse tethered to the mounting block, saluted glumly, and rode off.

The mistress collapsed on Tancy's shoulders.

His father's brandy mug was set by Billy's place at table that night, in celebration of the narrow escape. Miss Puddin allowed herself a small glass too, "just this once," as she did not normally indulge; it was not ladylike; but tonight she felt the need of a little something.

"At least we know now they're after you, Billy," she said. "Tomorrow you must take Stud and Swamp — they're the only ones to be trusted — and have them fix up the house on the other side of the woods pond, for a hideout."

"What house? There's no house out there."

"The duck blind, she means, Billy," Tancy blurted, forgetting herself.

The mistress said, "The duck blind, yes, it is well concealed. We'll make it snug and stock it with food and blankets so you can stay overnight, if need be. I'll put a boy to tend the road gap and signal us if that man comes again. It'll give you time to hide."

"Ah, I don't want to hide out in the duck blind, Mammy." The young man's broad face reddened with embarrassment and brandy.

"What do you mean?" Her tone was sharp. She hated it when he called her Mammy. He knew she hated it, and he seldom dared.

But brandy emboldened Billy. "Seems to me it's time I did my patriotic duty, Mammy, like everybody else."

"Everybody patriotic, hah!" she cried. "With the woods full of deserters and bushwhackers? You don't see anybody waving the flag these days, my boy. Why should they? There's precious little anybody can do now for the Confederacy."

"Well, do it for the Old North State, then. Defend what we've got left best as we can." He gave Tancy a suggestive wink.

Tancy dropped her head and moved closer to her mistress. She felt all at once uneasy. It wasn't like Miss Puddin to sit at table drinking with a man, even if the man was her son. And Billy wasn't himself, either, winking at her openly, preaching patriotism, boldly gulping his brandy.

Indeed, Billy was nearing an ignition point. He ached for action, and he didn't know what to do about it. He might have been a deserter himself by now, he brooded, one of those bushwhackers terrorizing the county; but as matters stood, there was no place for him among the renegades — no place anywhere, save at his mother's heel. Learning the business — what a fraud; it was Stud who really ran the mill. Billy felt asinine, pretending to keep books, when he had no head for accounts, no head whatsoever. Sighing, he reached for the brandy bottle.

"Billy!" His mother snatched the decanter from his hands. He gave her a long look. Trembling, she added a drop to his mug, and poured a drop more for herself.

She could not spare him, she told him in tones low and piteous. She was a woman alone, a widow, totally adrift without a man's hand to guide her. When he pointed out that other women survived widowhood — Elvira Shuford, for one — she denounced him for comparing her with that unwomanly woman. Did he not see that his mother was different, a genuine woman? She unfolded her fan.

"Yes, Mother, yes, little Mother," Billy hastened to agree. "I didn't go to upset you. My duty is here, I know that. Don't worry, I'll not leave you. We'll fix up the duck blind tomorrow, however you say."

So it was done. Quilts were carried to the duck blind, and emergency rations, and Billy drew off a large jugful of his father's brandy to fortify him against the cold nights he might have to spend there. His mother watched him carry away the liquor but said nothing to him, content to trade it for her larger victory.

"He's got his father's nature," she remarked to Tancy. "Well, I suppose he has to have some little pleasures. And he's not a child," she added with a significant nod. "A mere woman can't deny a grown man, when he sets his mind."

Mistress and maid alike observed Billy's daily trips to the duck blind thereafter, and the mother never questioned his flushed face and high spirits when he returned.

*

One by one the pigs disappeared. Julia hoarded pork rinds under her bunk for seasoning the beans. By the middle of March the last ham was gone; the smokehouse door sagged permanently open, nothing left to steal.

Probably never since the time it was built had this stout log storeroom stood empty. Tancy stepped inside it one day that barren spring to look around and to remember the bacon, fatback, side meat, that used to be racked to the ridgepole. The barrel they used for pickling pigs' feet lay dry and empty, scoured for its brine. Even the dirt floor of the hut, once tacky from dripping cure mixture, had been scraped up and boiled with water to recover the salt.

"Tancy."

Her whispered name sounded the alarm, but it was already too late. Billy's hand over her mouth smothered her cry.

"Watch," he ordered someone outside the smokehouse. With his free hand, he pulled the smokehouse door closed and hauled the latch chain inside. Only then did he release her, but slowly, and his upraised fist warned her not to speak.

Still she quavered, "Remember my finger" — foolishly, for

he knew that it had healed – and crooked it at him in futile appeal.

He brought his face close to hers. "Now," he breathed in her face. He smelled of brandy, onions and brandy. "Now, we'll take our time – take all the time we want."

His broad body blocked her from the door. She knew she shouldn't hope to escape, still she attempted a threat. "Miss Puddin knows I'm out here."

"Oh yes." Billy licked his lips and grinned. "She told me where to look for you."

He was lying! He must be lying. The mistress wouldn't have – wouldn't have – or would she? *He's got his father's nature,* Miss Puddin had said, *has to have some little pleasures . . . can't deny him. . . .* "Oh, Billy," she entreated.

"Undress," he commanded.

A deep thrumming sounded in her head.

"Come on, Tancy, don't make me fight you."

"It's a sin," she said feebly. She stood paralyzed. This was a bad dream, his hands unbuttoning her bodice. *Mother!* she wanted to cry out.

In haste, he ripped off her apron, yanked at the strings that tied up her underskirt and drawers, and burst out giggling at the silver spoons that hung about her waist. "The family treasure!" he exulted. When she moved to cover herself, he pulled her hands away and began fondling her breasts.

Her scalp prickled. "I'm cold," she whimpered.

He shoved at the heap of clothing. "Spread this stuff out, so I don't get my knees dirty." He giggled again.

"Billy, you mustn't, it's a sin," she pleaded. "Miss Puddin told you, I'm your *sister* – "

His open palm smashed against her mouth. "Don't you never talk like that to me, hear?" But for all his violence, he did not look particularly angry. He grinned moistly and pinched her cheek. "Hear?"

She turned her head aside and closed her eyes. Her mouth tasted of salt.

A choked cry sounded outside the latched door. "Billy! Oh, Billy, it's your mama — "

The man's head jerked around. "Stop that hollering! You know what you're supposed to do." But above his furious order there arose the wail of the mistress. "Billy, Billy, run! Billy, where are you?"

Billy swore.

"Hurry, Billy. They coming after you," whined the voice at the door. And all through the urgent pleading could be heard his mother's voice keening "Billeeee! Billeeee!"

He yanked the door open. "Who's coming?"

"Yankees. They down at the stable. Run for the pond."

Without a word he flung out the door and raced toward the orchard, heading for the pond, as Stud, the sentry, instructed. Tancy saw his crouching figure skim through the tender pink shimmer of young peach trees in bloom. In another moment he had plunged into the tall woods beyond, and she heard shouts coming from the direction of the stable. With a shock she remembered herself. She stood naked in the smokehouse, bare naked; and through the open doorway Stud stared at her nakedness. He muttered something she did not understand and shut the door between them.

She threw on her clothes. Outside the mistress screamed. Horses' hooves thudded past and men yelled. Tancy readjusted the girdle of silver about her waist. She cringed to think of walking past Stud, standing guard outside. But it had to be done.

Stud was gone. Just this side of the orchard, a man stood holding his horse and talking to Mrs. Gaither. He wore a gray, close-buttoned tunic and the soft peaked cap of the Confederacy. Captain Murdock. So it wasn't the Yankees after all. She did not pause to speculate where the shouting mob had gone, or where

Stud might be, or Billy. She went directly to the kitchen, and without a word to Julia rushed into the cook's sleeping shed. She knelt on the bunk, and cracking the shuttered window, watched what took place next.

5

THEY CAME OUT of the woods and through the orchard bringing Billy with them, laughing and joking and scuffling among themselves. Billy walked with an arm flung across the shoulders of an orange-haired soldier while with his free hand he swung his brandy jug in cheerful circles. With great good humor he presented the soldiers to his mother, who stood with Captain Murdock in the orchard; and Tancy heard him say to her, "They caught me square to rights, Mammy. Now don't you think we owe them a good dinner?"

Julia nudged wider the crack in the shutter. "Ain't that redhead one of the Ijames's chaps?"

Of course it was. No mistaking that flaming hair. Ansel Ijames was a Coddle Creek boy who, with his brother, had been among the first to enlist from that community. The brother had lost a leg at Antietam and returned to Coddle Creek; Ansel had gone on to fight at Gettysburg, with Colonel Early in the Shenandoah Valley, and with General Johnston during the long siege of Petersburg.

The soldiers gathered on the Gaithers' front porch, and Billy poured cups of brandy all around. Inside, Tish set the table with the silver, paroled for the occasion. Julia grumbled and added more dumplings to the pot in which an elderly hen had boiled all morning. When the guests took their places at table, Mrs. Gaither apologized for the meager fare; Gaithers had been on short rations for weeks, she emphasized; this was the *only poultry* left on the place after the last invasion of bushwhackers. The men, relaxed and jovial, missed her point entirely and fell upon the food.

"Chicken slick!" Ansel Ijames rejoiced, sucking on a thigh bone. "I ain't et chicken slick since I left Coddle Creek!" He sponged up gravy with a wad of dumpling.

"What is the news from Coddle Creek, Mr. Ijames?" Mrs. Gaither inquired, in an attempt to salvage the dinner party.

"Ain't had no lately word, ma'am," said Ansel. He picked his teeth with his fork and inspected something impaled on one tine before returning the tidbit to his mouth. "Pa never could write to speak of, and Ma done left out for Texas last year with Grand-daddy and them. Said she had her fill of Yankees *and* Pa. Ma ... !" He shook his head admiringly. "Granddaddy and them says it's not going to be no war in Texas, and they get to keep their niggers there."

"If I believed that," said Mrs. Gaither, "I'd leave for Texas right this very instant."

"You can't do that," said Billy merrily. "You got to keep a candle burning in the window for your soldier boy."

"Hear, hear!" The company slapped the table and set the silver dancing. Ansel and another soldier began singing a rowdy marching song. Mrs. Gaither fluttered her fan.

"Now, sir, let us discuss the time Billy will need before reporting for duty," she said, in a tremulous voice.

Captain Murdock lifted a finger and the music ceased. "He will have until directly after dinner, ma'am."

"That won't do; no, that won't do at all. You must allow him a decent interval to put his business affairs in order here

45

at Gaither's Mill, and, of course, he must be properly equipped — uniforms and traveling gear and so forth."

Captain Murdock cleared his throat. Dealing with Sherman, he said, took precedence over personal considerations. The battalion needed all the men they could get right now, and all the supplies. Billy and others mustered in the area would start immediately for Bentonville, riding their own horses, wearing their own clothes, packing their own food and blankets and such necessities as were feasible for an extended campaign.

"He can get him all the uniforms he wants after the first good battle," Ansel assured her. "This what I got on come from Shenandoah, off of a fellow that got in the way of a bullet — the best kind of cloth, and I never had to patch but the one hole." He clapped his chest.

Mrs. Gaither took a breath. To the captain she said urgently, "Mr. Gaither, when he was alive, provided a substitute for himself, and that was acceptable to the command, as I recall. I have an excellent slave here that you can take in Billy's place, a prime fellow, very strong and clever — "

The captain said his orders were to pick up Billy.

" — or two slaves, they ought to be glad to get two for one, wouldn't you think? Two of my best hands?"

The man shook his head and explained how it was. At the beginning substitutes were fine; they put them in the front lines and they fought like any good sons of the South. Lately, however, they were not to be trusted. They crossed over to the Yankees every chance they got and in the very same battle turned their guns against their former masters. "I understand the feeling of mother for son," he said. "In my job, I see many a sad parting — not the cheeriest of duties, ma'am, and I don't do it of my own free will."

He spoke with sincerity, but Tancy saw his eyes command those of his men in turn. They bent to their plates, spooning up Julia's boiled custard, and in another five minutes the captain rose, bowed to his hostess, and regretted that they must eat and run. While the sun was still high overhead, Billy rode off with the captain and his cadre. Stud rode with them, a little way behind, astride Mas Gaither's old riding mule, to wait on his young master at war.

Tancy watched them leave from the parlor window. It served Billy right to get caught, after the way he had trapped her in the smokehouse, and she rejoiced to see him go. Stud too; she despised him for staring at her nakedness. She hoped he would cross over to the Yankees, like the captain told about, so she wouldn't ever have to face him again. The idea of Stud crossing over gave her unexpected pleasure, and she felt a little softer toward him.

The party cantered out of sight. On the porch Mrs. Gaither threw her arms around a pillar and began to moan. "Oh, my boy. Billy, Billy, my precious boy."

Tancy went out to her. "Come in the house, Miss Puddin."

"He's gone," the mother lamented. "He's all I've got, and now he's gone!"

"He'll be back soon, Miss Puddin. Mrs. Shuford says the war is good as over. By the time Billy gets to where they're having it, it'll be all done with. You'll see."

"Oh, what do you know about the war? What do you know about anything?" Still she allowed Tancy to lead her into the library and to settle her on the chaise. All through the afternoon she remained there, while Tancy went back and forth with cold wet cloths from the washbasin to bathe the mother's swollen eyes. "My precious boy, he's all I've got," she would say, and her tears would flow anew. "It's awful. Awful!" She crushed her handkerchief against her lips.

Late in the evening, when Mas Gaither's little brass knee lamp guttered and began to smoke, she said with a sigh, "I suppose I'd better go to bed. I know I won't be able to sleep. It's terrible, being a woman alone and having no one to talk to."

Tancy began to sniffle. "You've got me, Miss Puddin. You can talk to me."

The mistress raised the lamp by its ring and started for the stairs. "You wouldn't understand. You're not a mother." Still, she laid a hand on the girl's arm. "You are a help to me, Tancy."

The words made Tancy weep out loud, which in an odd way comforted the woman. She leaned against her; Tancy's arm stole around her waist, and bound together in sympathy, together they went upstairs.

They spent the days that followed in fashioning a uniform for the absent soldier. Elvira Shuford cadged cloth and supplies for them from the military depot in Statesville. The new cavalry boots she brought went into a cotton basket packed with shirts, undervests, and drawers, a bought cap and belt, extra blankets, the pillow Billy had slept with ever since he graduated from the cradle. Nothing but the best for Billy.

On a limpid sunny afternoon, when a flurry of fading peach blossoms carpeted the orchard in imitation snowfall, Tancy sat sewing on the front porch beside her mistress. They were nearly finished. Tancy hemmed trousers, and Miss Puddin sewed a double row of brass buttons down the front of a jacket.

The mistress frowned at the work in her lap. Her eyes smarted, her neck ached; but of these discomforts she did not complain. She fastened her thread with firm stitches, looked off in the distance to rest her eyes, and beheld Stud coming up the lane afoot, leading a chestnut mare that was not Billy's Prettygirl. Across the saddle of the mare, like a turn of corn brought in to Gaither's for milling, hung a motionless form.

"Oh no," groaned the woman.

Tancy's heart surged with horror — or was that horrid relief? She had watched Billy ride off to war with vengeance in her heart. Now, this. *I didn't mean it,* she told herself miserably.

"No, God, please, God, no!" said the mother, panting.

48

Tancy took her hand and stroked it. "Miss Puddin – Miss Puddin – "

The travelers plodded up the road. Stud opened the gate and led the mare that was not Prettygirl along the graveled path and up to the porch. A little dog trotted in through the gate behind them and stood on its hind legs to sniff the dangling fingers of the corpse. Immediately it backed off and departed for the stable, with its tail between its legs.

Stud stood with sagging shoulders before his mistress. He wore a stained rag tied around his forehead. Below the band, his red-rimmed eyes glared through a mask of road dust. The reddened eyes blurred and tears runneled the dust on his cheeks. Stud touched the bloody rag binding his forehead, wiped his face on a sleeve. "He never suffered none," he offered, in a queer, hoarse voice.

"No!" Miss Puddin screamed. "Don't you tell me that! He's going to be all right. Billy! Billy! He's going to be all right! Help him down from there. Bring him in the house – he's going to be all right!"

Her shrieking brought Swamp and Julia from the kitchen. The two recoiled at the sight of the dead man, then Julia took over. "Cover him," she ordered the men. "You come inside, Miss Puddin."

"Help him down from there, I told you! Help him down!" the mistress raved.

The cook spoke soothingly, but guided the distraught woman firmly into the house.

Tancy, left alone on the porch, could not take her eyes from the misshapen lump that had been Billy. His hands hung heavy and blue below the mare's belly. The thick blond hair was clotted and stiff, like the pelt of some furred animal, warped out of character by rain and sun. His ears, she thought dazedly, his ears never stuck out swollen like that. Did they?

Inside the house the mother screamed, calling for her dead boy and imploring for him to be made well. She raged and screamed, and at times punctuated her cries with a sinister mirth. "Uh-huh-huh-huh-huh!" sounded the ghastly chuckle; and then the screaming would begin again.

The slaves in the quarters rushed up to the house. They slunk around corners and peeped through the shrubbery at the spectacle of Swamp and Stud struggling to lift Billy from the mare. The body had stiffened in an arch, but it retained enough flexibility to defy them. They would get him lifted up and then some part of him would give and the burden would thump back into place. With each thud, the mare staggered and heaved.

"You lift his legs on that side whiles I hoist his shoulders," Swamp directed Stud. "When we get him up clear of the saddle, Jake, you lead the horse out from under him." This latter was directed to a gangling youth who, braver than the others, had crept into the yard. Jake grasped the reins with the air of a conspirator. "Arright now, *ho!*" said Swamp, shoving against Billy's shoulders.

Julia reappeared on the porch. "What y'all think you doing?" she said furiously.

Swamp glowered. "Miss Puddin say bring him inside – "

"Never mind what Miss Puddin say, she out of her mind, can't you tell? And y'all out there – " She turned on the observers crowding around. "What you doing, snooping around up here?"

The slaves scattered, all except Jake, who, given the job of tending reins, hung on to them.

"Ride Mr. Billy down to the chillun's cabin," Julia directed, "and tell Minna I be needing her directly. I'll come to wash him and lay him out quick as I can leave the missus."

Swamp took the reins from Jake and backed the horse through the yard gate. Stud followed behind, as though drawn by invisible reins. His eyes did not meet Tancy's. He looked like a man sleep-walking. Once he stumbled.

"Go water that horse and give it some feed," Tancy instructed Jake. "When you get done, come back up to the house. I'll need you to take the funeral paper over to Mrs. Shuford." Her natural competence had surfaced; she was on familiar ground now. She was the one who had prepared the funeral paper for Miss Puddin, when Mas Gaither died.

Jake scuffed a bare toe in the gravel. He was not much younger than this girl ordering him around. "Who say?" he drawled, torn between rebellion and the honor of bearing bad tidings.

"I say. You want me to bring Miss Puddin out here to say it instead?"

Jake turned petulant. "Catch me on the road thout a pass, I get a whuppin."

"Nobody's going to whip a fellow with a funeral paper in his hand."

Still he felt like arguing. "Say it be a far piece to Shufords', and I don't know the way."

"Ask somebody, silly." But Tancy relented. "I know it's a long way, Jake, but that horse isn't fit to ride, and it's all we've got now. Somebody's got to run the paper over there. You're the fastest runner on the place, maybe in the whole county, and I don't know who'll get the word out, if you don't go."

Jake raced off importantly.

Little boys, thought Tancy. She went inside.

She paused at the door, beside the cotton basket filled with the clothing and comforts they had been assembling for Billy. The parlor was empty; Julia had taken Miss Puddin up to her bedroom. How strange the parlor seemed without Miss Puddin in it. Even the furniture looked changed, as though it had passed to a different ownership. The pendulum clock that stood between the windows hiccuped once and struck the half-hour. Only two-thirty. She passed through the curtained doorway into the library. Different in here too; the library had never really belonged to Miss Puddin. The ledgers, the newspapers, the writing materials all belonged to Mas Gaither, when he lived; and after him to Billy; and after Billy — to Tancy.

She seated herself boldly at the library table, laid out a sheet of letter paper, and uncapped the inkwell. "To my dear friends and neighbors," she wrote, "I grieve to inform you of the death of William Gaither III, of Gaither's Mill." She thought a minute and added, "He died bravely in the war."

And serve him right. The phrase leaped unbidden to her mind. She felt vengeful when Billy rode off, and now she must live with her remorse. Billy was her brother! He had taught her to read! Her eyes pooled and she leaned back, lest her tears blister the page. Sniffing, she continued. "Your presence is desired at the funeral — " Tomorrow? she wondered. Probably. Billy's body looked like it should have been buried several days ago.

Julia came down the stairs before Tancy could go up to inquire. "Tomorrow," she said, with the certitude of experience. "Tomorrow after dinner."

" — at the funeral tomorrow, after dinner. Yrs. respectfully, Cornelia W. Gaither."

Underneath this text she numbered ten spaces for friends and neighbors to sign. Mrs. Shuford would add more if she thought there ought to be more. She rolled the document and secured it with the black tape left over from Mas Gaither's funeral paper. Then she laid the official-looking scroll on the table, awaiting Jake's return.

6

ELVIRA SHUFORD came as soon as she received the funeral paper, bringing the stricken household prunes and incense. "Eat you some prunes along," she advised her neighbor. "Grief is mighty binding." To Tancy she said, "Bring your missus some brandy. Bring the whole jarful, and an extra glass for me."

When Tancy returned with the brandy, she dispatched her with the new uniform and boots to the children's cabin. "Your missus wants him dressed in these," said Elvira. "Soon as they get him fixed up in the coffin, fetch him to the parlor – that's where the viewing will be – and start burning incense. He bound to be stinking."

In the hollow below the big house, a dozen slave cabins straggled about an open space, like a shabby little village built haphazard around a green. One cabin larger than the others was designated the children's cabin. Here, while their mothers labored outside, children were cared for by Lessie, an ancient slave past her field years. Because of its size, the cabin was used for the women's evening tasks, carding and spinning, for prayer meetings, dances sometimes, and infrequent weddings. Here also the ceremonial progress to the graveyard began for the deceased of Gaither's Mill, on a high trestled slab of wood reserved for laying out the dead. Billy Gaither, age twenty, now occupied the slab.

"Don't he look natural!" Aunt Lessie admired Julia's handiwork, and Minna agreed, "Like he just sleeping."

They lied. Billy Gaither on the cooling board looked dreadfully dead. Julia had washed his hair and shaved his cheeks, but the new jacket had to be split up the back before she could button it around his swollen body. Those monstrous puffy feet could not be crammed into the stiff new boots. She had oiled and buffed his worn field boots and put them on instead.

"What makes his face so black?" asked Jake.

"The blood gone dark," Julia said. "They was so long on the road. Folks let him swap horses, Stud says, every time the one that was carrying Billy give out."

"Won't never see our little Prettygirl again, I don't spose."

"Won't never see none of our horses again, way things is going, horses nor mules neither." The woods corral had been emptied by Confederate troops the week after Billy and Stud rode off with Captain Murdock.

Jake continued to study Billy's face. "Preacher say if we good, we all turn white when we go to heaven." He snickered. "You reckon Mr. Billy ain't *gone* to heaven?"

"Where's your decency, boy?" Julia slashed at him. "Show your respect for the dead, if you got none for good white folks. Who learned you that ugly talk, I want to know? Tweren't from any raising of you that I done!"

"Where's Stud, Julia?" Tancy intervened to rescue the boy. He shot her a grateful glimmer and slunk out.

Stud was asleep, they told her. Fell down in his tracks when they laid Billy on the cooling board. They woke him up to make sure he wasn't dead too, but he just took a drink of water and went right off to sleep again, and they put him in his mother's cabin to recover. "Did you see his feet?"

"I didn't notice," said Tancy. "What about them?"

The poor fellow had walked the bottoms off his feet, Julia said; his soles were like raw meat. It would be a while before he moved around on those feet again. "No telling when he ate last. Maybe you like to bring him a little something for his supper?" she hinted.

Tancy said, "You take him something special, Julia. He'll appreciate it a lot more from you than he would from me." She dreaded having to face Stud again, and really, there was no need. Surely he had seen enough of her to last him for a while, that day in the smokehouse.

In the late evening the slaves all climbed the hill to the big house, to pay their final respects to the young master. Aunt Lessie shepherded the little ones. Round-eyed and fearful, uncomfortable in their clean shirts and tight braids, they trailed around the coffin, set upon dining-room chairs in the parlor. The atmosphere swam with smoke from the incense and the wavering candle flames. Although the women whimpered in their aprons, they gazed greedily at the pendulum clock, the figured carpet, the sofa on china casters; it was their first time in the big house since Mas Gaither's death. The men tugged at their ears and groaned. It was not so much that they grieved, but that grief was expected of them.

Stud, however, could not contain his sorrow, for he had genuinely loved Billy. Two strong men supported him as he looked on Billy's face. Tears washed his cheeks. He rubbed at the flow with his fist and his massive shoulders shook, although he made not a sound.

At last, Mrs. Gaither said crossly, "That's enough now, Stud. Crying's not going to bring him back." Elvira Shuford had urged upon her brandy enough to dull her own anguish. "I thank you for bringing him home," she said, "but I know you're tired. Go on back to the quarters and get some rest."

The men carried him out, to spare his mutilated feet.

55

Mrs. Gaither said to Tancy, "I want you to take Stud a glass of brandy. It'll help him sleep. Not too much, now; the cracked glass that I save my flower seeds in, that'll do. Put the seeds in my pin tray, and mind you don't spill any. I want the glass back, tell Stud."

But Stud did not answer Tancy's knock, and when she poked her head inside, she saw him already asleep on the rickety bunk in the corner. She slipped in to place the glass on the cut of tree trunk that served as table and returned to the big house.

Through the night she sat in the parlor with her mistress.

"I'm so tired," the woman confessed in the early hours of the morning.

"Go to bed, why don't you, Miss Puddin? You ought to rest. I'll sit with Billy."

"No. No. I can't do that. My son — my only child — I couldn't do that." She rose from her chair and peered into the coffin. "He doesn't look like himself. Bring me some siftings from upstairs. I don't want folks looking at him, all black in the face like that."

There were home cosmetics Mrs. Gaither had used for years, but she spoke of them in culinary terms, never as beauty aids. The vinegar and salt that lightened her hair were "seasonings"; dried raspberries "sweetened" her lips. "Maybe his skin just needs a little thickening," she said of Billy.

"I can't do it, you'll have to," she said, when Tancy brought her the powder.

Nervously, with a wad of cotton, Tancy applied the siftings. It wasn't the same as dusting Miss Puddin's papery skin, with Miss Puddin pinching her cheeks to bring up color, and blending in and feathering the edges. Billy's unyielding face felt like an unripe fruit, and the powder marbled his skin in the candlelight.

"That's worse yet." Mrs. Gaither plucked at her own face. "I won't have a viewing. I won't let them look at my handsome boy, all black and swollen. I'll have the coffin closed."

"You can't do that, Miss Puddin, that's what folks come to a funeral for, to see."

56

"Well, they're not going to see Billy. Oh!" She whirled and gasped, staring through the parlor window into the dark beyond. "They've come! It's the Yankees, come to get my spoons!"

"No, now, Miss Puddin, that's Uncle Swamp sitting out there, waking Billy. You come over here by the window and you'll see it's him, sitting there on the step. Nobody's going to steal your spoons with Uncle out there."

Her words only heightened the woman's agitation. She paced the parlor, twitching at the curtains, glaring into Billy's face, gabbling about the Lenoir woman who had been stripped naked by the Yankees.

Tancy was frightened. She desperately wished for Julia's help, but she dared not leave the mistress in her manic state. She walked the floor with her. She promised all she demanded. "Rest now," she begged the woman. "Rest for a while on the chaise in the library."

Toward daybreak, worn out, Mrs. Gaither finally dozed behind the curtain in the library. Tancy untied the spoons from around her waist and laid them in a row underneath the cloth that lined Billy's coffin. After that she perched, drooping, on a parlor chair to wait.

At the first brightening of the sky, she sent Swamp to fetch his tools. She roused and brought her mistress, ashen-faced and chafing her hands in the chilly April dawn, to say farewell to Billy. Swamp hammered home the last of the nails just as Elvira Shuford drove up the lane in her buggy.

*

There was food on the dinner table that day, more food than anybody had seen in months – ham and chicken and biscuits and cakes and every kind of pie you would ever hope to eat. The neighbors had measured up for Mrs. Gaither. They brought out of hoarding provisions that eclipsed all the wakes of local history, from Coddle Creek to Lone Hickory. Their offerings filled the dining room table. The sideboard and the pie safe were crammed, and Tancy helped Tish carry in the library table to take care of the overflow.

In the midst of plenty, both food and drink, before setting off for the cemetery, Mrs. Gaither asked Tancy, "Did Stud send my glass back?"

"He was asleep — "

"Well, go get it from him. He's not to think it was a present."

It was a queer afternoon. From the Charlotte road came the rumble of heavy wagons and voices and the clank of harness. Parties of soldiers tramped halfway up the lane, but seeing black crepe tied around the hitching post, turned back. Road noises mingled with the woeful phrasing of the deacon substituting for Preacher Tomlin, who had gone to minister to the troops at Bentonville. Elvira Shuford had failed to locate enough Fourth Creek men able to carry the coffin to the graveyard. Her field wagon and mule hauled Billy to his final resting place.

Only the slaves who dug the grave and who would fill it in afterward attended the ceremony. The others, presenting an air of muted holiday in the sharp April sun, gathered at Old Swamp's cabin.

"Miss Puddin wants her glass back," Tancy told Stud.

He sat on a rude bench by himself outside Alberta's cabin, still wearing the clothes he had gone to war in, had come home in, had slept in. His hair was still gray with road dust; his battered feet were now bound in greased rags.

"Well, shall I go get it?" Tancy persisted.

He shook his head sadly, though not in response to her question.

She entered the cabin. The glass of brandy stood on the make-shift stand untouched. She brought it out to him. "Miss Puddin says I must bring the glass back. You want to drink this first?"

She had plagued herself unduly about the smokehouse incident, she saw that. Stud did not seem to know who she was, much less in what state he had seen her then. He sat staring at the orchard

58

and fondling the wrappings on his feet. Yet at length he made room for her on the bench and took the glass she offered. He drank from it, and sighed, and began to talk.

You could hear the war going on, he said, the day before they got there, like a thundering that came through their feet. Earth shaking. Horses scared jumpy all the time. Then everything got still, and in some ways that was worse than the thundering. The captain called the men together and another captain or somebody high up came in and told them their orders, told them to eat their breakfast, and told them when he gave the signal they were to run over a ridge he pointed out and start shooting. Before they ever got a fire going good for breakfast, he gave the signal.

Billy left out of camp with his comrades, Stud said, but so far as he knew, none of them made it over the ridge. Ansel Ijames died, that red hair shot clean off. Yankee cavalry came pouring over and simply mowed them all down. Stud saw Billy grab his stomach and stumble. He was that close to him he could see his eyes, like they were looking for something, and his mouth worked like he was asking directions, "Where?" and he stood there for a little bit, with that asking look on his face, and then he sat down, with his mouth still working, and then he lay down.

Stud crawled over to him, but he already knew that Billy was dead. He couldn't see any blood, but there was a round hole like burned through his vest, and when he opened his shirt, there was a round hole like drilled there in between his ribs. Then horses began galloping over them and men were running and yelling, and Stud lay close to Billy, and they lay there for hours, hours, maybe all that day. It started raining, he remembered, and it rained a long time, and it stayed light a long time after the rain stopped; and all the time the shooting and the rain were going on, Stud lay there thinking how to pull Billy out of that war and get him home.

In front of Tancy and Stud, where they sat, Jake appeared suddenly and stood patting his hands together and dancing like some little chap waiting permission to speak. Stud, deep in his narrative, paid the youngster no heed. Jake whimpered his frustration and rushed away and into the children's cabin. When he came out again, Stud was explaining about the relay of horses that carried Billy home, but this time Jake interrupted.

"We free, Stud, Tancy! Scuse me for butting in, but I got to tell it — we free! They telling it out there on the road — the war's over and the niggers is free!" He performed an ecstatic dance and shouted, "Hi-eee!"

"Hush that!" Aunt Lessie ordered from across the way.

"Shh," said Tancy, but she asked immediately, "Who told you that? What makes you think it's so?"

"They all saying it on the road, Yankee soldiers and Federates, and they's niggers out there too, walking along like *folks,* without no passes nor nothing. Oh, it's true, you go ask for your ownself. We free!" Again he executed his exuberant caper. At the height of his jubilation he stopped short and smacked his forehead in wonder. "I'm going too," he announced. "I can walk right away from here and nobody tell me I can't."

"Don't be silly," said Tancy. "Where would you go?"

"I don't know." His face closed stubbornly. "I'm just going."

"You'd leave Aunt Lessie, that raised you? And Miss Puddin, that feeds you and gives you your clothes? You're still going to need food and clothes, you know, even if you are free, which I doubt. What are you going to do about that?"

Jake said uncertainly, "I don't know." But he looked somehow different; and he trotted away from them with a changed air, along the lane that ran from the stable past the big house, until it joined the Charlotte road.

They watched him go, Tancy, Stud, and the rest. A few of the others had caught the gist of his conversation, and the word passed instantly among them. The small groups congregated, murmuring. They doubted what Jake said. How could he know a thing like that before they did? Before Mrs. Gaither, even —

and who of all people should know a thing like that first, if not the mistress?

Tancy sat stupefied. Jake, a *chap*, walking off boldly, right in the broad daylight! How in the world was she supposed to tell Miss Puddin about that? She thought of how Jake had looked, walking away changed, vaguely different, and she figured out what it was that changed him: he was wearing boots. Jake was long ago entitled to his first shoes, but because of the war shortages he had never owned any. Now, in departing, he had appropriated the boots worthy of a gentleman soldier.

"He stole Billy's boots!" she exclaimed.

"All of us got something coming," said Stud unexpectedly. "If boots is all he wants – "

"What you mean by that?" Swamp moved in to hear what Stud had to tell. The rest closed in with him.

He told it as though it were a trifling incident that had slipped his mind. The war was over, he confirmed. They signed to end it somewhere around Durham Station. Stud got the word toward the end of his long walk home, and he knew it was true, because right away the roads started filling up with soldiers headed home and niggers headed somewhere else – they didn't know where – looking for something. He heard that every man who had been a slave was going to be given a start of land in freedom; forty acres, they said on the road; forty acres and a mule.

"We're all as free as any white man," said Stud.

"Forty acres?" Swamp sniffed. "Tell me another tale."

*

If Mrs. Gaither knew of the war's end, she did not mention the fact. Indeed, after the funeral, she scarcely talked at all, and Tancy, alarmed by her depression, kept trying to cheer her up.

"I brought your glass back, Miss Puddin, like you told me. Stud drank what you sent him and thanked you very kindly. I washed the glass out good and dried it and put your flower seeds back in it. You'll be wanting me to plant those for you out front, I spect."

"I spect," said her mistress listlessly.

But although the ground had warmed to perfection, she did not say where she wanted the petunias and where the zinnias. She took no interest in the mill's business and left spring planting to Stud's orders. Many days she did not dress, and Tancy no longer read to her in the afternoons. When the little maid carried up her tray at mealtimes, she would find the mistress sitting by the north window, which looked toward the family graveyard beyond the orchard.

"You want to walk up through the orchard this afternoon and see how good the new peaches set?" Tancy proposed.

The woman sighed. "They either did or they didn't. No. I don't have the strength for it."

Said Tancy, more boldly, "I could take some daffodils up, put them on Mr. Billy's grave for you."

The mother shook her head. Tancy worried about her. She picked at meals, not that there was much of anything good to eat, now that the funeral food was gone. She did not go out of the house, and when Elvira Shuford came to visit, she sent word downstairs that she did not feel like seeing her. Mrs. Shuford had not called on her since.

Then, in mid-May, abruptly one morning she observed, "Well, the old war is over, but the soldiers are still stealing everything they can get their hands on."

Tancy froze. Miss Puddin said it herself—the war was over! Would she also tell her she was free?

"What are you looking like that for? You knew the war was over, didn't you?"

"Yes'm," said Tancy meekly.

"I want you to tie some fresh crepe on the hitching post. It won't keep them from stealing out of the garden, but decent men will stay away from the house when they see black crepe." Later that day she asked for coffee, and stirring the parched corn brew with a pewter spoon, she was reminded: "I want you to hide my wedding spoons somewhere else, Tancy. The class of men out there on the road, it's a wonder they haven't stripped you naked already."

Tancy tried to think how to tell her the wedding spoons lay six feet deep, alongside her son.

"Don't tell me where," said her mistress. "No matter what they do to me, no matter how they torture me, I'll not be able to say where my spoons are, if I don't know, will I?"

"No'm," said Tancy.

7

IN JUNE MRS. GAITHER decided to remove the crepe bow from the hitching post. Soldiers no longer crowded the roads. But now, nearly every day, a company or two of pathetic blacks shambled up the lane looking for a meal, for shelter, for work. These hobo bands worked like a tonic on Mrs. Gaither's depression. Whenever she saw them coming, she would rush onto the porch, there to preside over their arrival.

"Y'all looking for something?"

One person usually spoke for the group. "Looking for our folks, ma'am. And grub. Reckon you can spare us a little somepen to eat?"

"You must be hungry, from the looks of you." The mistress would gently shake her head.

"Hungry, yes'm — mighty hungry. Two days thout nothen to eat."

"And no roof over your heads, I doubt. I imagine you'd be glad of some empty cabins in my quarters where you could sleep indoors for a change?"

"Yes ma'am! Oh, Lord bless you, ma'am. You got any work you like done, we be glad to work our keep."

Having won her audience, Mrs. Gaither would then proceed to lecture it, in a tirade that sickened Tancy. "No, I've got no work for you, you shiftless fools. How dare you come around here begging, when all you ever had came from your master? What kind of loyal do you call yourselves? Get off my property! Get away from here, before I sic the dogs on you."

Usually they slunk off. Sometimes they broke and ran. But one day a brave black woman stood her ground and yelled back: "Go on, sic the dogs! I got me a club here that broke a dog's back yesterday. You don't own us. You don't own *nobody,* not that little gal you're hanging on to there neither. She's free as you are. We're all free." She called out to Tancy: "We're all free now, sissy, ain't you heard?"

This time Mrs. Gaither retreated, shoving Tancy aside in her rush to escape the ranting woman.

In good spirits and at their leisure, the party turned back toward the Charlotte road, and Tancy with awe and delight watched them go. That woman actually talked back to Miss Puddin!

"Get yourself in here, girl," called her mistress. "I won't have you listening to trash. That woman is crazy. You know that, don't you?"

"Yes'm," she answered. But inside her head, she too talked back. *I'm as free as you are!* The same thing Stud had said. Tancy was beginning to believe it.

Stud had not mentioned freedom since the day of the funeral. None of the slaves had. Never having lived free, they were unsure of what it meant, afraid even to talk about it.

Ten days after the woman challenged Miss Puddin, an official visitor wearing the Union cap rode up the mill lane, tethered his horse, and announced himself to Mrs. Gaither. "From the provost marshall's office, out of Knoxford."

Mrs. Gaither's mouth pinched and her eyes slitted.

But he had met with cooler receptions than hers, and he recited in memorized phrases the purpose of his call. "Your servant, ma'am?" He indicated Tancy, who peeped from behind her mistress. "Paid servant? No? Are there other slaves – ex-slaves, that is – on the premises? Have you read them the Proclamation? With your permission, ma'am, I will read to them their rights as free persons; or if you prefer, you may read, so long as this is done in my attendance. Now how do you normally summon these persons, when the presence of all is required?"

Mrs. Gaither's icy stare meant little to him. He was civil, businesslike, interested only in seeing government orders properly carried out. Tancy was sent to Julia, who blew the hurry-up call on the cow's horn, three long blasts punctuated by two short.

The slaves of Gaither's Mill swarmed up the hill to the west porch, and the man standing there with Mrs. Gaither glaring read them what he said was their "freedom paper." The formalities of government language eluded the slaves. They shuffled in alarm, and the man translated.

"It means you're free now," he said. "You can come and go as you please. You can go someplace else and work, you can stay on here and work, if you and this lady agree to it. However, she, or anybody else you work for, has to pay you for working from now on."

Mrs. Gaither drew herself up very straight. Swamp and Lessie ducked apologetically in her direction, and Tancy realized that her own head bobbed too.

The deputy resumed his recitation. "As free persons, you are entitled to execute in your own behalf legal contracts for work. The Bureau of Freedmen has been established by the government for implementing your status as free persons. Offices of the bureau exist nearby in Knoxford and in Salisbury. You may apply to one of these offices for assistance. With contracts, for example. Also, the bureau can help you with transportation." He paused to see how his words affected his audience. Not one spark!

He recited more rapidly, without expression, "The bureau

may provide subsistence and shelter for such stranded persons as may require it. Facilities are limited, however. The bureau cannot undertake to locate missing persons, but at a number of offices across the state an informal system of registration has been initiated whereby separated families may be reunited."

The deputy droned the closing phrases of his speech with an eye on the gate where his horse was tied. His job bored him. All these ignorant slaves bored him. They stood around like posts while he told them the greatest news they could ever hope to hear, and they never changed expression, never gave the slightest indication that they understood a single word of what he said. Still, the bureau office in Knoxford was jammed every time he reported in. He couldn't account for it, seeing these blank faces.

He asked if there were questions. No one spoke up. He nodded to them, nodded to Mrs. Gaither, and departed.

Mrs. Gaither watched him canter out of sight before she relaxed. The motionless slaves watched her. She dusted her hands.

"There. That's over with." She ran her gaze slowly across the faces turned up to hers. "I suppose you're wondering what he meant by all that talk?"

Nobody answered her, but Swamp shook his head.

"It isn't as bad as it sounds," she assured him. "Nobody's going to make you leave Gaither's Mill. He said himself you were allowed to stay on here, if you wanted to."

Crazy Nell began smiling and babbling, and the mistress smiled back at her. "Scared you, didn't he, Nell?" she said. "Don't you worry. Miss Puddin won't let him send you away from here."

Swamp said fervently, "Praise God!"

"Why!" she exclaimed, warming up, "Y'all are *my folks*! It would break my heart if I was to lose you! Mr. Gaither always vowed we'd not sell our slaves, and you know it yourselves, we never did."

"Never did," said Swamp. A murmur ran through the crowd.

"Never sold, never bought, except when one of our slaves

married outside. Last time was when the master bought Minna from Overcash's, for Risky. You haven't forgotten that day, I spect, Risky."

"No ma'am, I sure don't forgot it. I thank Master till yet."

"I thank Master too for my LeRoy, rest him!" cried Aunt Lessie, beginning to weep. Aunt Lessie's LeRoy had died of pneumonia the previous winter.

"Yes, sister, rest him."

"Rest Master too. Lord, rest him." Aunt Lessie and Swamp began a sing-song between them.

"I can see how you feel," said the mistress. "I feel the same way myself. Y'all go on back to doing what you were doing before the deputy came, and don't worry anymore about who's going to take care of you. Miss Puddin'll take care of you, like she's always done, and we'll go on together – please God – just as long as He sees fit to keep us here on this earth."

"Amen," said Swamp.

"Amen," said Aunt Lessie.

"Amen! Amen! Amen!" shouted Crazy Nell. "Hallelujah, praise the Lord, have mercy!"

"Now, Nell, don't go getting excited," said Mrs. Gaither. "Minna, you take Nell to the quarters before she gets to hollering. Get her to help you with the quilts. That'll calm her down, maybe."

"Lord have mercy! Lord have mercy!"

Minna looked about her for help. Her three children danced in a line on their way back to the quarters, but at their mother's bidding they turned back and seized Nell's hands. They ringed up and circled, piping a childish chant.

"Mercy?" said Nell, ready to be diverted. She stumbled eagerly through the paces of their ring game.

> *Rain, rain, rain all around,*
> *Ain't gonna rain no more.*

What did the blackbird say to the crow?
You bring rain, and I'll bring snow.
Caw! Caw! Caw!

"Caw!" Nell crowed delightedly.

Smart, Tancy thought. Minna was like that, sensible and easy — slow, Mrs. Gaither complained. But Minna had a way of getting what she wanted. If she wanted it bad enough, she could probably get her children to sing down the rain. The summer was heating up fast this year, too fast for the season's late planting. Mrs. Shuford said the drought had to break soon, otherwise she wouldn't make a crop.

Rain, rain, rain all around,
Ain't gonna rain no more.
I had an old hat and it had a crown —
Looked like a duck's nest setting on the ground.
Quack! Quack! Quack!

*

When night fell and the Carolina damp came down, the slaves built a bonfire at the center of their clustered cabins, and their singing and shouting surged and spurted in the spongy air. Inside the big house Mrs. Gaither sat at the dining room table and flicked a fork at the cornmeal dumplings on her plate. They were getting cabbage from the garden now and three kinds of beans and enough squash to throw at the birds, but as yet they had only the promise of a pig from Mrs. Shuford, who had successfully defended her pregnant sow against the foragers; and the chicks of their meager June brood were still in fluff.

Tancy watched the flicking fork. "The way Julia fixes dumplings, you don't hardly miss ham hock," she suggested.

"I most certainly do miss ham hock," said Mrs. Gaither tartly. "Stud hasn't even brought us a fish, weeks now. If Billy was

69

alive, either we'd have fish on the table or else he'd learn Stud how, and I don't mean with a fishing stick." The dining room window glowed, and the mistress turned like a sunflower toward the light.

Tancy said quickly, "Stud thinks somebody's robbing his trotline, is why. Because, see, he can't run it very often now, because of Uncle Swamp's broken leg, and because, see, Stud's got to mind the mill — "

"Oh, mind the mill! I could mind the mill with my dresstail caught in the door — what is that hollering out back anyway?"

"Frolic," Tancy soothed, "probably just a little frolic."

"Little frolic? Who gave them permission? You go tell them put out that fire and quit their yelling right this minute." Tancy edged toward the door. "And pull down the window before you go. I don't have to listen to fools while I eat."

By the time Tancy reached the quarters the fire and shouting had subsided. Figures moved back and forth among the cabins and in groups on the lane to the Charlotte road. Against the evening sky she thought she recognized the silhouettes of Risky and Minna and their three children, walking with bundles in their arms.

"Who all's going there?" she asked Stud. The big fellow stood alone, teasing some smoldering twigs with straw pulled from an old mattress. "Isn't that Risky and them going yonder?"

"Yo, it's them." Stud flung a spray of straw, and the remnant embers flung back flames.

"Mistress says for you to put the fire out, she never gave permission. Where are they going this time of night? She never sent anybody a pass."

"They leaving. Don't need no pass no more. Pass time run out, didn't you hear the pro marsh say, up there? We free now. Freeee!"

"Bye, Stud." Horace brushed past with his cat in his arms.

"Coming with us, Stud?" That was Bob, leaving in lockstep

with Blind Bob. The two had been tandem friends since they were shirttail boys, perhaps through the kinship of their names. Whenever you saw Bob, you saw Blind Bob yoked behind him, walking with his hands on his friend's shoulders.

Tancy exclaimed, "Stud! You aren't planning on leaving. Good as old Mas was to you? Miss Puddin without anybody to run the mill?" And recognizing that she would be the one to carry this news to her mistress, she begged, "Please don't leave us, Stud."

The man's eyes glistened. "You want me to stay?"

She said skillfully, "Poor Miss Puddin, first old Mas and then Billy, and now you fixing to leave her. Uh-huh! Well, go on, leave, I can tell you mean to. Burn the place down, you're free now."

Stud hunched miserably. "Our ma bound we going to hunt up the rest of our set," he pleaded. "Me, I'm the only one big enough to help Muh till her find Pappy."

He began glumly kicking dirt over what remained of the fire and she left him, well pleased with herself. After all, Miss Puddin wasn't the worst mistress in the county. Still, though she did not realize it, the stealth and ferment of the quarters had infected her. Custodian of the night's secrets, she sped up the hill to the kitchen, and on an impulse burst in upon Julia, sitting on the throne of her high kitchen stool and emanating her queenly power as cook.

Tancy stopped short, guilty of trespass. "Oh, Julia. There you are."

The cook had always been able to make her feel guilty of something. Of anything! Now she inclined her regal head. "What you want?"

What did Tancy want of Julia? She could not explain the yeast that worked in her. Instead she cast about for some reasonable errand that might have brought her to the kitchen. Luckily, the house bell that hung over the door clanged. "Miss Puddin wants her tea," she invented promptly. "Where is Tish? Why hasn't she brought the tea?"

Ominously Julia said, "She gone."

"Before supper's over? Where's she gone?"

"Where she want to, I spect. Ain't for me to mind where she gone to."

"Well, how is Miss Puddin supposed to get her tea, then?"

"That ain't for me to mind neither. I ain't no waiten maid." Julia glowered at the tea tray.

"Course, you aren't," Tancy placated. "You're the cook! Cook isn't expected to cook and carry in too. Here, I'll bring it myself, long as it's ready. Oh my, mint tea, doesn't that smell good!" She lifted the tray awkwardly. She was not accustomed to serving. She elbowed open the slabwood door and froze as the cup chattered in its saucer.

Majestically the cook descended from her stool and held the door for Tancy's passage. "Tish gone to hunt up her folks," she said without expression. "You can tell Missus what you want to."

In the open passageway between kitchen and house, Tancy paused, a reluctant bearer of bad tidings and makeshift tea. Why was she to blame for all this? She wished — she wished —

"What happened to the tea Elvira Shuford brought me?" Mrs. Gaither knew perfectly well their neighbor's funeral packet of real tea had barely got them through Billy's wake. But it gave her something to complain about, and she felt entitled. The war was over, they ought to be getting tea by now; she needed tea, after all she had been through; why couldn't she at least get coffee, answer that?

Tancy assured her that they would get some any day now. Somebody from closer to Charlotte would bring in tea or coffee along with his grain to swap for a milling at Gaither's, more tea and coffee than they would know what to do with. The peddler would come around again too, with tea and sugar and salt.

Maybe he would bring cloth as well. Miss Puddin could have a new summer dress to wear Fourth of July.

"No, I can't, you know I can't; I'm in mourning," her mistress denied, and she began to weep.

It was too much. Tancy wept with her. She no longer thought about Billy in the smokehouse. She remembered instead her childish playmate in the sunbonnet his mother made him wear when they played outdoors. He was sweet then. They made frog nesties with their bare feet in the sand. They linked arms and played Sail Away Raleigh; they gambled at Hully Gully with chinquapins, and they rode the willow trees down on the branch. He was dead, that little boy in the bonnet, dead before breakfast a hundred miles from home. No more frog nesties.

"Stop your bawling," said Mrs. Gaither. "It's hard enough for me without you blubbering. Ring up Tish to light the lamp — plague! What's wrong with the girl, did Julia say? Starting up her monthlies, I suppose. She's old enough."

Tancy brought flame on a splinter to the parlor lamp, and within the circle of its heartening light, the mistress speculated pleasurably on when the peddler might come around once more with his goods, and what kind of cloth he would bring. For all she knew, the fashions had changed entirely since the last drummer turned in at Gaither's Mill three years ago. Not that it mattered, for she intended to mourn Billy — and Mr. Gaither too — the rest of her life. "But I do need a new mourning dress," she said. "It isn't respectful of Billy, this rusty old thing I've worn ever since Mr. Gaither passed. Look at it. You wouldn't even call it black, would you, now?"

Elvira Shuford had worn a new locket to Billy's wake, the mistress mentioned. Where did that woman find a locket in these times? And wasn't she wearing a new bonnet as well, at the funeral?

"Oh, it makes me too sad, sitting in here," she exclaimed. "You may as well come brush out my hair, Tancy, though I know there'll be no rest for me this night."

In fact, after they retired, the mistress in the high poster bed, the maid on her floor pallet, Mrs. Gaither promptly fell asleep and began to snore. Tancy it was who lay awake, thinking of those departing figures, Stud's exultant "Freeee!" and the crackle of straw on the bonfire. . . .

At some time in the night, the mistress reached down with her fan and rapped the girl out of her quirky slumber. "Whuh — whuh — ?"

"Answer me, when I speak to you," the woman commanded. "Was it Henkels that brought the molasses pie or was it Allisons?"

"Ma'am?"

"When Billy died, stupid. Who brought the molasses pie?"

"Mrs. Henkel did, best I remember it."

"No, had to been the Allisons. The Henkels have been out of flour since Christmas, and besides, that was a good pie. They haven't ever had any kind of a pastry cook at Henkels'."

"I spect you're right, Miss Puddin."

"Well, and who brought the jug of brandy? Seemed to me like that was in pretty poor taste, bringing brandy to a widow woman. Been different if there was a man in the house to bring it to."

"Yes'm."

"Fetch me a drink of water, girl. I knew I wouldn't sleep a wink this night."

What time was it? The night sky framed in the bedroom window told Tancy nothing. Waiting beside the bed for Miss Puddin to hand back her glass, she wondered how far they had got by now, Minna and Risky, Horace, Blind Bob. The daring of it! She lay down again on her pallet, filled with envy and dread.

8

A SENSE OF WAITING FOR SOMETHING woke Tancy the next morning. In the bed above, Mrs. Gaither smacked her lips and groaned and turned over toward the light. Sun thrusting in the window struck a dazzle from her mirror. The mistress would not sleep long with that in her face. The horn blowing the slaves to work usually woke her at first dawn.

The horn. That was what Tancy dreamed of waiting for, its summons. There was not the drift of wood smoke either, rising from the kitchen, or the robust smell of hot grease that accompanied Julia's cooking. Why wasn't Julia cooking breakfast? Tancy crept from her pallet.

"Tancy," said her mistress drowsily.

"Yes ma'am."

"Is that my breakfast?"

"No ma'am. Julia didn't bring it yet, and Tish, she's sick — "

"I know, I know, quit telling me that. What time is it anyway? It's so light outside."

"I'll go find out."

"Well, find out about my breakfast, while you're at it."

The girl ran barefoot down the stairs in her nightshift. Nobody except Julia, she thought, to catch her in her shift.

And, of course, there wasn't even Julia. The kitchen door sagged derelict on its wooden hinges. The big iron stove was cold. The door curtain to the shed where Julia slept had been pulled down; the shelf of honor that displayed her enamel pitcher was vacant; in fact, the shed was empty of all her clothes, her doctoring herbs, her quilt, of Julia herself.

"Julia!" Tancy called once, but she knew she called only for the consolation of hearing her name. No more Julia. She felt hollow and tremulous. She sat down on Julia's bunk and stroked it and whimpered, the way Jemmy had stroked his mother's footprints in the lane, the day Mary was sold away. Why did she grieve? She was scared of Julia, didn't even like her much — yes, she did! she thought guiltily. She had to love her — Julia was almost like a mother to her.

Out on the walkway she scanned the quarter for some sign of activity. The cabins looked derelict too, already abandoned shacks. There was no laundry stretched on the fences to dry, nobody sweeping the dirt yards, no children ringed up before the huts to prance and chant their play songs.

"Go look in the quarters," said Mrs. Gaither, when Tancy reported the cook's absence. "She's probably down there doctoring Tish. Or if you see Minna, tell her to come fix my breakfast."

"Maybe Minna's not in the quarters."

"Well, of course she is, idiot. I told her to wash all the winter quilts. That's enough to keep her busy there two full days, slow as Minna is." She looked at Tancy suspiciously. "What made you say that? Do you know something you're not telling me?"

"No ma'am, no, I don't know anything. Not anything. Just, they might think, because the provost man said, and if they worked, they might think they'd be paid for it, I was thinking maybe they — "

"Think! Think!" the woman shrilled. "Who told you a nigger

76

could think? You go get Julia like I told you to, before I give you a good brushing."

Tancy grabbed her clothes and ran.

The quarters were not deserted, after all. Crazy Nell came out and gobbled a greeting. The front of her dress was already soaked.

"Where is everybody?" Tancy asked her.

Nell smiled her tender, open-mouthed smile. A filament of drool spun from lip to bodice.

Tancy could hear Swamp shouting, and she hurried across to his cabin. Swamp and Nell had not lived in the same cabin together for many years. Jemmy shot through the open door as she approached, and the old man swung to the threshold on crutches he had fashioned out of forked branches. "Come back here with my pipe!" he yelled. "You little snot, ain't I gonna learn you! I ast him bring me my smoke," he said to Tancy. "Stead he take my pipe and run with it. When I get ahold of you!" He shook his fist at his grandson and chomped his lips furiously with stumps of rotted teeth.

"Em fools done left, honey," he said to Tancy. His old eyes watered and he stared aggrievedly toward the high road. Most of them had departed after dark last night, the others early this morning. They were on their way to Salisbury, he said, to Knoxford, to Statesville, the world.

They were going to register with the provost marshall, with the Freedmen's Bureau, they were going to give themselves new names, whole names, and some of them were going to take paying jobs, and some of them were going to get land and farm it and make money that way. Stud said the bureau would give them forty acres and a mule to start out with.

"What do they know," Swamp raged. "They never knowed nothing cept what old Mas told them. They think the beero will help them — huh! They crazier than Nell to believe that. Nell ain't got sense enough to look after her own grandchild."

"Jemmy's your grandchild too," Tancy reminded him. "They've gone to look for their people," she said gently. "Didn't you do the same when you were young? I've heard you brag about running off to your first wife, and how they couldn't beat you enough to keep you from her."

"No, they couldn't," he declared, cheering up. "Cut my hide so bad they had to lift me up in a sheet — my back's pieded yet. Called me Swamp from all the times I hid out in the bottoms. But I knowed it was wrong," he explained virtuously. "When Mas give me Nell, I come to my senses, and after that Mas ain't had no better hand than me. Jemmy! You hear me, you bring me back my pipe!"

Jemmy stuck the corncob in his mouth and imitated his grandfather's limp on a crotched stick he had found in the woodpile.

"Don't you mock me!" Swamp shouted. "I beat you to death if you mock me!"

Jemmy's shirt barely reached his belly button. He was naked from the waist down, and his capering scabbed legs bore the marks of many a scrape. He was not much older than four, but already in that baby face sparkled the clever eyes of a rogue.

"Jemmy," said Tancy, "Uncle Swamp needs his pipe. Give it back to him now, and let's you and me go up to the big house and get us some breakfast."

He was clearly tempted. He paused to listen, though at a distance, and he studied her shrewdly.

"Give it back. You can't come with me if you don't give it back. Uncle Swamp *needs* his pipe. It's his playpretty. What if he took your playpretties and never gave them back?"

Jemmy contemplated. Won over, he sidled up and offered the pipe. Swamp grabbed his arm and began beating him with his crutch.

Tancy cried out, "Stop it, Uncle Swamp, you'll hurt him! He's only a little boy."

The child was screaming, and the old man, yelling too, ignored her shouts, and she had to wrestle the crutch away from him. Swamp was still a vigorous man, but with his broken leg, he was no match for her. "You don't realize how strong you are," she scolded him. "You could have killed him with that club."

"I'll learn him *or* kill him," the old man panted. But he allowed her to help him to a bench and sat mumbling as she peered into the swing kettle hanging in his fireplace.

"Did you eat yet?"

His rage rekindled. "That's just it! I was fixing to feed *him*. Me, I done et whiles he laying in the bed, and I like to have my smoke after I eat, but what I do, I go to get him his mush, and what he do, off he runs with my pipe. Huh! He gonna find it make a long hungry twixt eatens, he mess with old Swamp."

Jemmy wound himself, snuffling, in Tancy's skirt. "My's hungry," he whined.

The old man spat. "Stay hungry awhiles. Might be you learn something from it."

Tancy thought fast. "There's nobody to cook for the big house, Uncle," she said. "Let me just carry this mush up to Miss Puddin. I'll take Jemmy with me so you can have your smoke in peace."

He grunted. "You can take him and keep him, for I don't want him."

Mrs. Gaither received the news of her slaves' departure calmly. It was almost as though she had been expecting them to go. "They'll be back," said she, with a disdainful poke at the mush Tancy set before her. "Where are they to go? Who would feed them? There's nobody but me going to give them clothes and take care of them when they're sick. They'll come dragging back pretty soon, you'll see, and maybe I just won't take them back; then you'll hear them pray!"

"Who'll do the work, Miss Puddin?" Tancy was thinking of the mill, and of the washpot full of wet quilts down at Minna's.

"Girl, there isn't but two of us left to do for! You'll have to see after my clothes, now that Tish is gone, and the meals. Naturally I don't expect fancy cooking from you."

Tancy said, alarmed, "Miss Puddin, I can't even cook *plain*."

"You'll have to learn," snapped the mistress. "A girl your age ought to know cooking and housekeeping too. *I* certainly did when I was your age." She pushed forward her plate. "You better bring me some more mush. A body that takes over a house has got to have a little something in her stomach to work on."

Tancy rushed out to the kitchen, glad for the opportunity of checking on Jemmy. He perched bare-bottomed on Julia's biscuit block with the bowl in his lap, and he greeted her with a melting, mushmouthed smile. "More!"

She lifted him from the block and dusted off his floury behind. Later in the morning she slipped off to the lumber room and rummaged in the trunk where Billy's baby clothes were stored until she found a faded little pair of pants that she hoped her mistress would not recognize. She put them on the boy and taught him the function of that important flap in front. He spent the rest of the morning buttoning and unbuttoning.

"Now, where did that one come from?" said Mrs. Gaither, when she caught him peeing on her petunias. "Bad enough they left me with that old cripple and the half-wit. Who's supposed to be minding that child?"

"Uncle Swamp; except it's hard for him, with his broken leg, and he isn't used to minding chaps — "

"I'm not taking any young'un in at the house, you understand that."

"No'm, I just gave him his little something to eat, was all."

"None of us'll get our little something to eat, if the garden doesn't get rain pretty soon. You there, boy! Don't you know better than to open your britches like that? Nasty! Nasty!" The mistress descended upon Jemmy, scolding and shaming. But she also drew a bucket of water from the well and carried it to the garden and set him to reviving the wilted tomato vines, one gourdful for each plant. "That's the proper way to water the garden," she told him. "You know where the privy is, don't you?"

When he nodded meekly, she said, "All right, then. Open your britches in the privy when you have to go, but I don't want to catch you making nasty in my flowerbed again, you hear me?"

"Yes, Miss Puddin, ma'am," said the boy, with the sincerest of smiles.

She left him intent on the marvelous new assignment. To Tancy she said, "That one might make a hand, one day." From her, it was high praise. It struck Tancy that Miss Puddin might come to care for charming Jemmy. She knew what it was to rear a boy, after all, and he needed rearing; and if this little fellow could distract her from her grief . . .

"I'm not taking him into the house," warned the woman, reading her mind.

To Tancy's surprise, Mrs. Gaither really did know about housekeeping. She knew how to fire up a cold stove gradually, so as not to crack its plates, and she could feel with her hand inside the oven and tell when it was just right for baking. She knew how to spot a stain, so that it didn't set; and she made beautiful bluish starch that was utterly free from lumps. Before dinnertime she showed Tancy the right way to sweep, but she ended up doing it herself, because she said Tancy was too slow and raised the dust besides.

Tancy thought, So I raised a little dust. She imagined herself working in a town somewhere, doing an interesting job that paid money. She shuffled the flatirons for her mistress, from stove to ironing board to stove.

"Now, this is the way you're supposed to iron gathers," said Mrs. Gaither. "Tish never could iron gathers like this." She showed Tancy the right way. Who needed servants? Not she! But her energy flagged under the day's labors, and she fell into bed early that night, without a word about Jemmy, spraddled on Tancy's pallet.

Tancy straightened the boy's limbs and settled beside him. He was so little! But he was sturdy; she loved the muscular look of those scabby, little-boy legs. She cupped her body about his and put her lips close to his ear. "Jemmy's a good boy. Miss Puddin loves Jemmy," she whispered, to seed the thought in his dreams.

*

The crawdad holes dried up down on the branch. The ripening blackberries, wizened and flavorless, scarcely warranted picking. Water still filled the mill reservoir, however — three creeks fed it — and Miss Puddin sent Tancy to padlock the sluice gate. Anybody that wanted milling done would have to call first at the house, she said. But no customers came the entire month of June.

And the neighbors did not call. Miss Puddin complained about that, but, in fact, every day brought household crises that left her no time for visiting. Crazy Nell came up from the quarters early in July slobbering and wailing and displaying a cruel burn along her forearm.

"Now I've got to do the doctoring as well!" said Mrs. Gaither. She wrung salve from the aloe plant and spread it on a rag and dressed the arm. The wound healed quickly, but Nell refused to cook for herself after that and crouched by the kitchen door at mealtimes, wheedling and pointing at her afflicted arm.

Swamp too came up every day and moped around, hoping for a handout. To him, Mrs. Gaither said, "Isn't that leg of yours getting any better? Seems to me time you ought to be walking on it some and helping out."

He started telling her how the pain kept him awake every night, how he was afraid the bone was melting instead of mending, like had happened to Risky's pappy; how he couldn't be expected to get better when he couldn't get any good food to eat. . . .

"Oh, do spare me your tribulations," she said. "I don't feel so good myself, worn to a frazzle, and I'm just about to smother in this heat."

Jemmy leaped to offer her her fan, which he played with whenever she wasn't looking.

"Why, thank you, Jemmy," said Mrs. Gaither. "There's a likely boy," and to Tancy, "Get this little feller a sugar tit."

Jemmy looked mortified. He was too old for a sugar tit! But he did accept the cut of sugar cane that Tancy peeled for him, and graciously heard out her praise. He acted so grown up, Tancy told him. Miss Puddin *loved* clever boys like Jemmy, that brought in kindling so smart and pulled the weeds along the fence. "I bet Christmas come, Miss Puddin's going to give Jemmy a good present."

He leaned against her and sucked his sweet. "Are you my mammy?" he inquired innocently.

She pressed him closer to her. "Your mammy went away with the trader, honey, don't you remember?" He looked both confused and disconsolate, and she tried to set things right for him. "You and me, we have Miss Puddin for a mother, and she takes care of us."

He gazed at her trustfully. "Us go find our *real* mammy."

"Maybe, someday." She told herself she really would go, when she felt she could leave Miss Puddin. When Miss Puddin got someone to help with the work. When the neighbors remembered their duty and came to call on her again.

The very next day they had a caller, a timid knock at the back door. Tancy crossed her fingers that it would be Elvira Shuford come to pay her respects, but of course it wasn't. Mrs. Shuford was front door company.

A barefoot girl with nappy hair and a dingy striped apron stood on the porch. She pouted at her feet and she simpered at her pert, round belly. When she saw it was only Tancy, she straightened and lifted her mouth to a point, beaky and bold. "Come looking for Bob."

"Who is it?" Mrs. Gaither rustled up behind her maid. "What you want, girl?"

She dropped her head. "Bob," she whispered.

"Say again? Speak up! Bob? Lots of Bobs in this world. Which Bob you looking for, girl?"

Faintly, she said, "Gaither's Bob."

"Well, you came to the right place, but you're a little late. In more ways than one, looks like to me." She surveyed the girl's midriff. "Bob's gone. Sneaked off with the rest of them a while back. There's nobody left here cept the no-counts."

The girl did not look up.

The woman said, not ungently, "So, I guess you'll have to look somewhere else for him."

Still the girl said nothing, still she stared at the floor. On the floorboard at her toe, a tear fell and blurred into the furry wood.

"There, don't cry over Bob. I wouldn't waste my time on him, if I was you, not that one – chasing after a different girl every week. I hate to say how many different places I wrote him out passes to, Shufords and Goforths and Rankins and I don't know where all else. If you're smart, you'll forget about Bob. There's too many other girls he's giving the eye."

The girl stirred. "Not my Bob. He blind."

"*Blind* Bob, you mean? Why didn't you say so at the first? Hmm. How come a healthy gal like you to take up with a blind feller?" When the girl did not respond, "Whose nigger are you anyway?"

"Marse Johnson's, from Coddle Creek."

"You a fieldhand there?"

"No, I been a house girl mostly."

"Can you cook?"

"Yes – well, some. Mistis learnt me to do a little bit of everything."

"What's your name?"

"Patsy."

84

"Patsy, *ma'am*, Patsy. . . . I tell you, Patsy, Blind Bob cut out of here must be a month ago or more, but it's my belief he'll be running home before long. The niggers won't ever make a living without their white folks."

Patsy fingered her apron.

"So, seeing you're in the family way, and it's my nigger that's to blame, I'll take you in till he straightens himself out and comes home. Of course, I will expect you to do a little cooking and a few things around the house to pay for your bed and what you eat."

Patsy opened her mouth in a speaking way, but no sound came out.

Mrs. Gaither said sharply, "All I'm trying to do is help out. It appears to me like you could use some help. What do you say?"

Patsy studied her toes. "Progoe say we sposed to get paid for working," she mentioned.

"Oh, provost, provost—I am so sick of that provost I could puke. It's not fair! Mr. Gaither paid good money for our slaves, not even counting their training for years and doctoring them and such. I'm willing to let the niggers go free—well, it's the law now, whether we're willing or not—but I say they've got to work out what they cost us in money first."

"Yes'm," said Patsy. She turned to go.

"Wait a minute," said Mrs. Gaither. "I don't have any cash investment in you, so it's only right for you to get paid for the work you do. I'm prepared to give a dollar a week for a good house girl. Mind you, for those wages I want a good week's work, no laying out on account of your condition; you understand that."

"Yes'm," said Patsy, with a beautiful smile. A dollar a week!

"There's a room off the kitchen where my cook used to sleep. You can stay there for now. Tancy will bring you a sheet for the bed and a quilt. Extras like that, of course, will have to come out of your wages."

"Yes'm," said Patsy.

A dollar a week. Tancy had never been inside a store and could not guess what a dollar would buy. Mas Gaither, when he bought the Womack property at auction, said it cost him a dollar an acre for the land, so she knew a dollar was a lot of money. She felt jealous of Patsy, the wage earner. A mere girl, but she had *asked* for her rights, and she had got them. Imagine! She didn't look to be any older than Tancy herself.

Patsy was, in fact, not quite sixteen, Tancy learned, when she carried her the worn bed linen the mistress provided. Blind Bob had been her regular feller for more than a year. They had agreed to marry back at Christmastime, and he had knitted her a lovely pair of stockings for a wedding present. He could do anything with his hands — weave, knit, spin, plait — and he played the quills and sang beautiful songs made up by himself. All the girls at Johnsons' were envious of Patsy's talented feller.

And now they were going to be together always, a married couple. As soon as Patsy learned about freedom, she had set out to look for her man. It had taken her a long time, walking, not knowing the way from Coddle Creek; and the records at the Freedmen's Bureau in Knoxford were a jumble, so she had to wait around for days for that office to direct her. Her name was written up in Knoxford, Patsy boasted.

Two years younger than Tancy, already a wage earner, *and* written up in Knoxford!

"Marster wrote me on a paper and progoe put me in his book, in Knoxford. Progoe say we can call ourselfs any name we want in freedom.

Tancy hugged the bed linen, jealous but curious. "What name did you pick out?"

"Patsy Gaither is how I'm wrote in the book," she said airily.

"But you're not Gaither's — you're Johnson's."

Patsy said with dignity, "Gaither is my matrimony name. Progoe say if me and Bob jump the broomstick, we just as married as anybody. Maybe us get us a matrimony license though, when Bob come. You can do that now, you know, get a license wedding. You don't have to ask your old miss can you do it. Us don't have to ask mistis *any* permission."

Tancy attempted condescension. "Here at Gaither's, Miss Puddin's more like a mother to us than a mistress."

Patsy nodded wisely. "I've heard that before. Mostly I heard it from white folks, though. Me, I got my own blood mammy at Coddle Creek, and I ain't deny her for any white mother."

Tancy flung her bundle onto the bunk. "Fix your own bed," she told the other girl. "I'm too busy to stand here listening to you brag." To her chagrin, the bell in the kitchen jangled at that moment.

Patsy grinned her pointed, beaky smile, a bird ready to peck. "Yeh, you better go, your *mammy's* calling."

Tancy fled in frustration to the big house. She found her mistress yanking at the bell pull and peeping through the parlor curtains. "Somebody's turned up the lane," she said joyfully. "Tell Patsy to put the kettle on."

"Miss Puddin," said the girl, near tears, "I've decided to go find my mother."

"It wouldn't be Elvira Shuford, though, riding astride."

Tancy said weakly, "I just thought I'd tell you first. . . . ."

"No, it's some dirt farmer on a mule," said the mistress in disappointment. "Go out on the porch and ask what he wants."

The visitor was a shambling poor white in mud-stiff homespun, come down from the back country. He had ridden all day hunting a place where he could get a turn of corn ground. They were broken down at Crater's Mill, he told Tancy, and the folks were gone and the mill boarded up at Lone Hickory. His mule was saddled with the grain sacks, and he carried a hen tied by its feet as payment for milling.

A hen! They could eat off a bird that size for a week.

Swamp stumped on his crutches down the lane to the mill and

supervised as Tancy opened the race. He stood by gumming his lips and growling as the farmer helped her drag the grain upstairs to the buhrs, and he hollered at her and criticized the meal that slid, fine and clean, through a trough to the bagging room.

Later, by lamplight, she opened Mas Gaither's ledger and entered the transaction in her round, firm handwriting:

Jly. 23   Abel Underwood . . . . . 1 turn corn

and in the column headed Income, she entered:

. . . . 1 good hen.

She went over the pages Billy had scribbled on and spent a satisfying evening correcting and straightening out the mess he had made. Patsy, clearing the supper table, goggled at her each time she passed the library door, but Tancy ignored her. Let Patsy wash dishes. Let Patsy see who did the writing in this house.

"I've been thinking, Tancy," said Mrs. Gaither at bedtime, as the maid brushed out her hair, "that I ought to pay you something for working the mill. We'll be getting a deal of business, I spect, with Lone Hickory and Crater's both out of service. If milling comes in the way I think it's bound to, and you do your job right and keep the books on it, I'll see that you get your dollar a week, same as Patsy."

"Miss Puddin — " said Tancy.

"I mean what I say. Here's a dollar to start you off with. That's not any dead reb stuff I'm giving you, mind, that's solid silver." She paid the coin into her maid's palm.

Not since Tancy forfeited her two pennies to Julia had she held hard money in her hand. How far might this dollar take her!

Mrs. Gaither observed her maid's reaction in the mirror. "Now, about your mother," she said. "There's no telling where she is, after all these years. I'll ask around, and you can be saving your money, and then when the right time comes, you can go hunt her up, with my blessing. I just don't want you sneaking out in the dead of night, the way the others did. When you leave Gaither's Mill, I want you to leave like folks. Promise me that."

"Yes'm," said Tancy.

You don't have to ask permission, Patsy had said. Miss Puddin was never going to give permission, Tancy knew that. Miss Puddin would try to buy her off or make her feel guilty about abandoning the mistress who had been so good to her.

But Patsy was here to do the work now, and Miss Puddin still had Swamp; and there was Jemmy to keep her company. Tancy could go. She had money; she could go.

And she didn't exactly lie to Miss Puddin, she told herself, plotting on her pallet, with Jemmy moist and sweet in the curve of her body. All she promised was not to sneak off in the dead of night. So she would sneak off in the dead of morning instead, before the mistress awoke; and wouldn't that be the exact same thing as telling the truth?

9

IN THE MILKY BLUE DAWN LIGHT, Tancy plaited her hair securely over the silver dollar and tied a turban around her head. She sat gazing for a while at her mistress asleep in the poster bed. When she allowed herself one last look at Jemmy, she discovered him lying quietly there and watching her. She put a finger to her lips, pantomimed that he should go back to sleep, and crept from the room.

In the library she opened Mas Gaither's ledger for the year 1849 to read once more the entry she knew by heart:

9/9/49 – Lulu sold to Thad Shuford $600

My mother, she thought; I wasn't even two years old.

Before she could replace the ledger, Jemmy eased through the curtained doorway, trailing his shirt and beloved trousers. Tancy knelt and held him close. "Too early for getting up, honey," she hummed in his ear. "Jemmy go back to bed. Jemmy go sleepy-sleepy, and don't sturb Miss Puddin."

Jemmy was not in the least sleepy. His eyes sparkled bright and knowing. "Us go find our mammy now," he chortled.

"Shh!"

There would be no persuading him to go back to bed; she saw that. She dressed him and handed him his nightshirt. "Why don't you go out to the kitchen and get us some breakfast?" she suggested. "There's some left of that skillet bread Miss Puddin made yesterday, on the table, under a towel. We could eat it out on the porch."

He trotted obediently to the back door. She saw him through it and made for the front. She let herself out silently and raced down the lane.

At the high road she paused to consider, feeling jittery about leaving the only home she had ever known. Never had she traveled farther from the big house than to that mill standing before her. She was afraid. If she went back to the house right this minute, she would still be better off than she had been yesterday, richer already by a dollar, and with the assurance of a dollar a week from now on. Furthermore, the mistress had promised to ask around for her mother.

But Miss Puddin knew very well that Lulu had been sold to Thad Shuford. She didn't need to ask around. How stupid did she think Tancy was anyway?

"Tancy!" Jemmy came panting down the lane to her. He carried the loaf of skillet bread wrapped in his nightshirt. He padded up to her and inquired innocently, "Us going to eat our breakfast here?"

"Oh, Jemmy." She couldn't think how to get rid of him now. Furthermore, she realized, she hadn't the heart to. She took his parcel from him. "I hope you didn't wake Patsy up?"

He ignored her and looked delightedly up and down the big road. Not for him her doubts; he jigged impatiently. "Where us going to eat our breakfast?"

"Down that road apiece," she answered, pointing. And they headed south together on the high road to Charlotte.

For a long time she kept looking behind them, half expecting to see Mrs. Gaither coming to fetch them home again. Jemmy ran ahead to see what wonders awaited them around the bend and ran back to report. The sun came up. It was going to be another hot day, hot and cloudless, like the procession of days that had dried up the piedmont all through July. Tancy stopped watching for her mistress and began to enjoy herself.

They stopped twice, first to eat some skillet bread, and later on to drink from a stream that a low bridge crossed. Here they sat for a time and dangled their feet in cool water and talked of the happy day when they would find their mother. Jemmy persisted in believing that one mother was sufficient for the two of them, and when she tried to explain, she only succeeded in confusing him.

"You be my mammy," he decided.

She described Mary, to make his mother real to him – skinny little Mary, with hair long enough to pin up in a biscuit on top of her head.

"Biscuit!" Jemmy giggled.

"And you loved her so much, you kept looking down the lane after the speculator took her, and you stayed there by her foot-prints till it got dark, before you went back to the quarters."

Jemmy stuck his thumb in his mouth. Was it cruel to tell him these things? But she wanted him to know! She didn't want Mary to be a secret, like Lulu, that he would be almost afraid to find out about. She wanted him to know everything – everything! – so he could be free.

What would she have done without him? She sang him the songs she knew as they walked along, and taught him to count his fingers. He brought her a pretty stone from the road, a flame of butterfly weed, and a dead tortoise, stinking mightily. She thanked him gravely for each gift. They were good companions. They belonged together.

Toward noontime she had to carry him for a distance. He had grown tired from the long morning's walk, and cranky, and she plodded along, parched and hoping to find water to wash down the dry skillet bread. Before her wearied senses could warn her, they were overtaken by a man on horseback. She clutched Jemmy tighter and leaped for the ditch, but it was too late; the rider reined his horse up beside them.

"Where you youngsters heading?"

Tancy could not make her tongue work, but Jemmy piped sociably, "We going to find our mammy."

"Got any idear where yez'r lookingg?" Idear. Lookingg. Even in her fright, Tancy marked the queer way he spoke. He wore ordinary homespun and a blue slouch cap. "Know where ya ma is?" Blue Cap probed.

"Shufords'," Tancy blurted, and then panicky, "But maybe she's not there anymore, it was a long time ago, years, I was just a baby and I don't remember, not anything." She babbled wildly, in despair at having told what she probably should have kept secret. For all she knew, this man patrolled the roads routinely, looking for criminals like her and Jemmy, and would deliver them right back to Gaither's Mill.

Another idea came to her. "We're really going to Knoxford. Our mistress sent us," she stressed, "to register at the bureau in Knoxford."

"Yez'r going the wrong way for Knoxford." From his judgment seat in the saddle, he pondered her case. "Tell you what," he said, "they's a big old ammalance hauling a crowd of folks to Knoxford from up Snow Creek way. They maybe five, six mile east of here. Let's us catch you up with them. Might be they know is yer ma at Shufords', or if they don't know nothing, yez can ask at the bureau when you get there. Save you rambling the roads."

He dismounted and swung Jemmy to the saddle. "Hang on there, sonnyboy, till me and sis gets up. Now, sis, you put ya foot in the stirrup and throw ya leg acrost."

She did not know how to refuse. In her world there was no white person whom she was privileged to refuse. Her bare toes reached high for the stirrup. His careless hands gave her bottom a boost, then he quickly sprang up in front of her and settled Jemmy upon the pommel.

He wheeled his horse and they galloped back in the direction they had come from. Jemmy shrieked with delight. Tancy clamped herself to the stranger. She had always wished she could ride a horse, it looked so effortless and floating. But this wasn't anything like floating! The horse's rump pounded hers; she could not get a purchase with her knees; her toes flapped, useless, with every jounce. She clung desperately to the man in the saddle. Her arms were being torn from their sockets. She would be killed!

"Stop him, please make him stop," she entreated Blue Cap; but with her mouth scrubbed into his coarse shirt as she clutched him so tightly, he probably could not hear her; at any rate, the horse galloped onward. "Oh, Miss Puddin," she moaned, and closed her eyes to await the end.

"There she is," the man shouted. Opening her eyes and craning her neck, Tancy saw ahead of them a large cargo wagon drawn by two mules and jammed with people.

A cheer went up from those in the wagon. The conveyance halted and the horse with its riders reined in alongside.

There ensued a conversation between Blue Cap and the ambulance driver. Tancy grew conscious of many eyes looking her over. With her arms around Blue Cap and her skirt hiked, she just knew she looked all hugged up and indecent. She tugged at her skirt and heard the driver declare that he wouldn't take any more passengers; the ambulance already held more than two mules ought to pull, and they still had a long way to go.

"Most of it's downhill," Blue Cap argued, and the people in the wagon added their pleas. "Pray, boss! Take 'em in, pray!" "They ain't but chirren," they reproached him. "Can't leave chirren out by theyselfs on the road."

The driver relented. "But these two are the last," he roared at his passengers. "I ain't stopping for no more, hear?"

94

"No more," a woman mammoth of bosom agreed, and "No more, no more, no more," chanted the others.

A white man had spoken out in Tancy's behalf! The crowd had spoken out for her too – her head swam with the audacity of it. She began to believe a little in freedom.

Her legs went limber, when Blue Cap lifted her down, and she staggered in the road. Jemmy screamed to remain on the horse. He clung to the pommel, but Blue Cap plucked him loose and with a laugh tossed him into the ambulance. "Good luck, folks!" he called out and rode off, free and easy. What an incredible encounter, what a world this was outside Gaither's Mill. Freedom!

The wagon bed of the ambulance rode low on tall spoked wheels. Hands reached over the side to help Tancy aboard, and once again they were on their way.

"Going to find our mammy," Jemmy squealed, "that the speckle-lady stole!"

"Where you mammy, hon?" asked the mammoth woman.

"Shufords'," said the astute Jemmy, and Tancy, braver now, confirmed it. "Widow Shuford's."

The woman bellowed, "Anybody here from Shufords'? This little gal's looking for her mammy – what's you mammy's name, hon?" Tancy told her, and again the woman called out, "Lucy, or Lulu, anybody know a Lulu belongs to Widow Shuford?"

Nobody claimed knowledge of Lucy or Lulu.

"Birro'll find her for you," the mammoth woman assured Tancy.

They were a happy crowd in the ambulance. All stood; there was only a seat for the driver, but no matter; they were riding in the freedom chariot, and they sang it out joyfully.

> Riding in the chariot.
> Yes, riding in the chariot!
> Riding in the chariot, Lord, Lord!

Twice that afternoon they overtook foot travelers; true to his word, the driver declined to pick them up, but as each group came into hearing distance, the passengers called out to them.

"Where y'all going?" "Who you looking for?"

The answer would come back timidly, fearfully, "Dunno."

"You can tell us; you free!" the mammoth woman could cry. "You know you free, don't you?" She would continue to question and advise as the wagon trundled onward: "Looking for you folks? The birro find em for you in Knoxford. Foller us, that's where us going, birro find our folks for us. Birro gonna give us forty acres."

"And a mule," added a baritone voice.

They arrived in Knoxville in the heat of the afternoon, hungry and thirsty. The skillet loaf had been wheedled away by their companions as soon as Tancy made the mistake of unwrapping it. Few of the riders had thought to bring provisions; nobody remembered water.

The ambulance pulled into a town whose size and grandeur overwhelmed Tancy. From listening to Mrs. Shuford, she knew there would be houses and shops, but she had never expected to see anything like this. The street where they entered was lined with huge, white-painted dwellings, houses with deep porches, houses with fluted columns, houses three stories high. And she had once thought the Gaither house was the finest!

"Lordamercy, looka them houses!" exclaimed Tancy's bosomy friend.

The riders in the ambulance admired in silence. In front of an elegant brick mansion, a small black boy sprinkled water from a bucket onto the powdery dust of the wide roadway.

"You there, boy!" The large woman leaned outside the wagon to speak to the lad. "Reach me up a drink of that water." She held out her hand for the bucket. The little boy stopped sprinkling and the woman snapped her fingers. "You hear what I say, boy? Reach me the bucket else I get you a good licken."

The little boy stepped close to the ambulance. "Here." He flung a handful of water into the woman's face and raced madly away.

"Oh!" The riders breathed in horror. Where they had come from, children respected their elders. This was something new.

The woman sputtered. "If that's how town folks act, take me back to the country."

They drove past two narrow cross streets before they reached the center of town. There the driver pulled up his mules in front of a large square brick building. Close by stood a wooden two-story hotel, with galleries above and below, and a horse trough at one end of the ground-floor porch. Tancy's fellow passengers tumbled out of the ambulance and rushed to the trough.

"Wait once, you folks," called the driver. "They got drinking water inside the bureau."

They ignored him. They shoved one another to get at the water, and having drunk, reassembled in pairs and groups to gawk at the sights of the town.

Tancy gawked too. There were stores on both sides, all the way down to the next cross street, a dozen stores, maybe more. There were two hardware stores and two saloons, not counting the hotel, which also advertised a saloon. There was a barbershop and a drugstore, with all sizes of jars on its shelves, and a grocery store. A tiny shop next to the hotel bore the sign Millinery. In its trim little showcase, a fantastic pink bonnet perched on a hat rack. A card at the base of the hat rack advised the price of the bonnet: $1.50.

Tancy wanted that bonnet the minute she saw it. She *wanted* it! Even Miss Puddin had never owned as pretty a bonnet as this one. Pink roses decorated the pink straw crown. A veil of green netting muffled the bonnet's curved brim; and on the underside of the brim were fastened green ribbon streamers for tying under the chin of the lucky owner. And it cost just $1.50!

"Inside's where you sposed to go, miss," the ambulance driver was saying.

Tancy heard his voice without hearing what he said. She had a dollar of her own plaited into her hair. A dollar wasn't enough. Would she have the courage to walk into that shop, even if she had enough money to buy the bonnet? She felt all sweaty, thinking about it.

"Miss."

She finally heard the driver addressing her, calling her Miss — her, Tancy!

"Inside there." He directed her toward the large brick building.

A huge sign painted on the face of the brick had been white-washed over, but thinly, so that Tancy could easily read the original words through streaked film:

KINCAID BROS. — SLAVES BOUGHT AND SOLD

She grabbed for Jemmy and took a step backward.

"This is the bureau," the man said, gesturing. Sure enough, beside the door, a paper marked Freedmen's Bureau was tacked up on a notice board studded with the tacks of many previous posters. Tancy swung Jemmy onto the high concrete stoop of the building and vaulted up after him.

The man snorted his amusement. "Steps around here on the side." There they were, two narrow steps crowded into the corner so that she hadn't seen them from where she stood. Tancy felt ashamed of the way she had hopped up on that block, like a country girl that knew nothing of side steps; but the fact that the steps were there, like the man said, and the sign too, like he said, gave her enough confidence to walk inside. Jemmy clutched at her skirt.

Inside was a long, dim hall where many black people milled around a water barrel. They spoke in subdued accents; they were worried-looking people, scared-looking; but one old woman, bent almost double, crooked a finger at Tancy. "This the right place, hon." She was the only cheerful-looking person in the hall.

Tancy looked back for more encouragement from the driver, but he was lounging against the concrete stoop unconcernedly picking his nose. "Find us a drink of water," Tancy said nervously, and nudged Jemmy toward the barrel.

There must have been half a dozen enamel dippers hooked around the rim of the vessel – another first for Tancy. She watched the others to make sure it was all right before unhooking a dipper and filling it for Jemmy. Nobody disputed that, so she unhooked another and filled it for herself. Water from the front yard well at Gaither's Mill had never tasted so good as this town water did, drunk from a town dipper, shaped like a gourd dipper, but stylishly made of gray speckled enamel, like Julia's pitcher.

At the back of the building, a door with glass in its upper half admitted light to the hall. A forbidding flight of stairs ran up one side of the hall to some gloomy region above, posted against trespassers by a chain fastened across the stairs. A sign suspended from the chain further stressed No Admittance. There were more signs above office doors on the side opposite the stairway: Provost, Transportation, Subsistence, Contracts, and signs whose lettering Tancy could not make out at the far end of the hall. It was all very official looking and intimidating.

A crowd of people emerged all at once from the office labeled Subsistence, and a uniformed guard at the door swung both arms in a great, beckoning arc. "Next!" he bellowed. "Step smart, folks; step smart."

The crowd around the water barrel surged toward him. Tancy felt herself propelled from behind. Before she could save herself, the throng jostled her into the office, and forward, until she headed a line that formed before an ink-stained wooden table where a white woman wearing a loose linen cap sat writing in a ruled ledger similar to Mas Gaither's daybook.

"Jemmy!" Tancy called wildly. The rush had separated them. Miraculously, he appeared at her knee. Somehow he had wormed his way to her through the forest of legs inside the room. They locked hands thankfully.

"Name," said the woman in the linen mobcap. "Name, please, and state your need." She tapped the butt of her wooden penstaff on the table.

"Lulu," Tancy squeaked.

"You'll have to speak up, child. I can't understand when you mumble."

Tancy tried again and got it out. "Lulu."

The woman dipped the nib of her pen and wrote. "Lulu. The last name?"

"I don't know, ma'am. Shuford, I spect, but I don't know for sure."

"You don't know your own last name?"

"Oh! Yes ma'am. It's Gaither."

"I see. Lulu Gaither."

"No ma'am. Tancy. My name's Tancy Gaither."

The woman drew two precise lines through Lulu and wrote above it, Tansy Gaither.

Tancy silently corrected the spelling. Tancy with a *c*, not an *s*. Aloud she explained, "Lulu is my mother."

The woman nodded. "I understand now. Subsistence for your mother, yourself, and your little boy."

"Jemmy's not my little boy. He belongs to Mary."

"For self then, and mother," said the woman.

"Ma'am?" The mix-up scared Tancy, but she was more scared of the woman writing down something officially, permanently wrong.

"I beg your pardon?"

Tancy faltered, "I don't know what I'm supposed to say."

The woman drew a small perfect star in the margin of her ledger. She said neutrally, "Food. You want food for you and your mother."

"I don't know where my mother is!" Tancy wailed. "Maybe

she's at Shufords', but I don't know where that is either." She poured her story out in a rush. She told about Lulu in Mas Gaither's ledger, and about Mary. She told about Jemmy following her down to the road, and she told about the horseman and the ambulance and the long trip to Knoxford; and all the time she was talking, the woman in the mobcap drew perfect small stars in the margin of her ledger.

"You have come to the wrong office to locate your mother," said the woman when Tancy had finished (☆), and she warned her that the bureau had nothing but an informal register of missing persons (☆☆), which was just experimental, really (☆☆☆☆☆). Mr. Emory, the uniformed guard outside, would direct Tancy to the proper office (☆☆). Miss Michaels — a hand-printed sign propped on the table told her name: Lydia Michaels, Subsistence — wished she could help Tancy, but her job was to authorize meals for hungry people. "Mr. Emory, can you come here, please?" called Miss Michaels. "This young lady — "

"We're hungry too!" said Tancy desperately. "We had some skillet bread, but the people in the ambulance ate it." It suddenly became important to keep contact with this woman whose mobcap looked like the one Miss Puddin wore when she cleaned house, whose ledger looked like Mas Gaither's daybook.

"Never mind, Mr. Emory," Miss Michaels told the guard. She prepared to write again. To Tancy she said, "I don't like to rush you, but others are waiting." They were, too, the whole office filled with them. They stood humbly waiting their turn. Miss Michaels said, "The little boy's name?"

"Jemmy Gaither," said Tancy hurriedly. "If we could get some supper, and a place to sleep just for tonight — " She understood the ledger now, what all those columns were for. She had always been able to read upside down, and out of the corner of her eye; she had always had to.

"James Gaither." Miss Michaels wrote it out.

"No," said Tancy, watching. "Jemmy. J-e-r-e-m-y."

"You can spell!" said the woman. "Can you write too?"

"Yes ma'am."

Miss Michaels turned the ledger around and handed her the penstaff. Tancy wrote it out for her in her clear round handwriting. She wrote the address for herself and Jemmy: Gaither's Mill, Iredell County. Taking a chance, she checked the *Supper* column, and for good measure, *Breakfast*.

Miss Michaels did not challenge her. She smiled slightly and said, "I could use a girl like you in this office. Would you be interested in a job here? Doing this sort of thing?"

Tancy could not answer. She had already exceeded her limit. She managed to nod, however, and Miss Michaels handed her two paper tickets, which she said could be exchanged for some supper out in the backyard. She said she would speak to the provost marshall about hiring Tancy after she finished today's registry, "if you're sure you're interested?"

Tancy found her tongue for that one. "Yes ma'am!"

"Then you and Jemmy go out and eat, and I'll talk to you about it after dark." It seemed that they worked until sundown, just like at Gaither's Mill.

Mr. Emory led Tancy and Jemmy along the hall and through an enclosed back porch and down a flight of wooden steps to the yard. A huge black man was out there using a hoe to stir something in a huge black pot. Mr. Emory told the man to feed these two new ones, Miss Michaels's orders. The cook hoed out portions of strange, leathery meat stewed with hominy onto two tin plates.

Tancy led Jemmy over to a paling fence to figure out how to eat their supper without any spoon. Jemmy put his face in his plate before she could stop him. Tancy wouldn't eat with her fingers. She might be a country girl, she decided, but she didn't want anybody making fun of her for it. Right away she found a piece of bark she could pull loose from a fence paling to scoop with. Jemmy scraped potlikker off his chin and watched her. He looked around until he located a bark spoon for himself, and they finished their meal tidily, watching the crowd of people entering the backyard from the bureau building, from the side street, from the cellar.

It was while they were discussing what they should do with their empty plates that Stud climbed out of the cellar of the brick building and walked up to them. "Tancy?" he said wonderingly.

10

JEMMY TACKLED STUD at the knees. Tancy exclaimed, "Stud!" and flung her arms around him. The big fellow staggered under the double embrace but returned her greeting so warmly that she disengaged herself and said primly, "I'm surprised to see you here."

"Muh been laid up with the itch, reason how come we still here," said Stud. His family had been in the jail for over a month.

"In jail! They put you in jail?"

Jail was what they called the holding station at the slave market, the man explained, before freedom. It was in the cellar of the Freedmen's Bureau, and now the bureau used it to shelter folks that hadn't any place to go, or that were sick. They made you wash before you could sleep there, but everybody they took in got food and medicine and a place to sleep; and sometimes clothes. Stud himself was wearing good heavy boots with leather laces.

He led them on a tour of the premises, beginning with the tub of water where two women washed the supper plates. If you didn't eat everything on your plate, you had to scrape it and wash it yourself, even though the women were paid to do it for you. The food wasn't what anybody was used to, but most everybody ate it.

"I thought it tasted pretty good," Tancy said sedately.

Stud looked all around before responding. "Taste Yankee," he confided. "Sometimes they give you crackers stead of bread – "

"What's crackers?"

"Dry – like thin, dry – " He shook his head. "You'll find out. They give crackers a lot. And mix vegetables, oh, my lordy, they don't have no flavor whatsoever, cook without any fat meat or anything make it taste right."

Stud showed them the jail, where he said Tancy and Jemmy would probably spend the night. Barred cells lined the walls of the basement. Inside the cubicles were mounds of straw, used for bedding.

"Burn the straw and wash the whole place out twice a week," said Stud. "They pay a gal three bits a day, and she don't do nothing but that one job."

"Miss Michaels says the bureau might hire me," said Tancy. "Just think, if they paid me three bits a day – " Already she was scheming to buy the pink bonnet.

Stud said bitterly, "They all time give out jobs to the women, and it's men that's got families to look after that needs the work. If I could get me a paying job – "

Tancy said, "Why don't you ask Miss Michaels? They must have jobs for men. They had a man out there cooking supper."

"Cooking," he sneered. "That ain't no job for a man, not for no real man."

Miss Michaels, all smiles, came looking for Tancy before sundown, and Stud left discreetly. Good news! Miss Michaels reported. The provost had given her a voucher for Tancy.

Voucher?

"It means we can pay you to help us register," she explained. "I'll take you inside to Supply now, before it closes. You've still got to have a bath and – did you bring any clothing with you?"

Tancy looked at her bare feet.

"Never mind. We'll find something. Everything you've got on has to be fumigated first anyway."

Miss Michaels could not promise how long Tancy's job would last. Congress had allotted no money for running the bureau, she said, and what little they got through the military had better be used up before the army changed its mind, in her opinion. "They'll pay you twenty cents a day, six days a week. I hope that's all right."

A dollar twenty! It sounded good. More than Patsy was earning. In less than a week Tancy would have enough, together with her silver dollar, to buy the pink bonnet! "Yes ma'am," said Tancy. She would have answered the same to any white woman who spoke to her, but it was different with Miss Michaels. She had begun to trust this woman.

In the supply office, Miss Michaels rummaged through used garments piled in a bin marked *Little Boys*. "Here, these ought to fit Jemmy. Try on these shoes. I'll find some of my clothes for you to wear; we're almost the same size. Both of you must bathe before you sleep in the dormitory — that's regulations for all of us. Because of disease and vermin, you understand."

They hauled warm water from the backyard to the dormitory upstairs, and Tancy and Jemmy washed behind a burlap curtain that concealed a metal tub and two dome-lidded chamberpots. When they emerged, clean and self-conscious in the strange night-clothes, they saw a form lying on the bed at the far end of the attic. "Teacher," Miss Michaels whispered, swiveling her eyes drolly. The bureau's Yankee schoolteacher always retired early.

The dormitory had been used for accounting and record storage by the slave merchants who owned the building, Miss Michaels said. She propped the door wide to create a draft and raised the three windows overlooking the street as high as they would go. The army had cleared out the former attic and furnished it with iron camp beds and a water bucket to accommodate its female employees. A large coal-oil lantern hanging from an exposed rafter lighted the area.

The whole place — the burlap curtain, their nightclothes, the sheets and blankets, their own skin now — smelled of chemicals. Miss Michaels said they would quickly get used to the odor.

She pulled off her mobcap and a rope of brown hair uncoiled to her waist. "You and Jemmy will have to share this bed next to me, until I can requisition another one. Heaven knows how long that will take, if they ship it from the army depot."

Tancy looked dubiously at the exhausted Jemmy, asleep in the middle of their bed. Was there room there for her? The spindly iron cot looked barely adequate for one.

Miss Michaels tied her hair back with a string and climbed into her bed. "Turn that knob base counterclockwise when you're ready," she directed. She closed her eyes and crossed her arms over her chest. Her lips moved.

"Ma'am?" said Tancy.

Miss Michaels continued to murmur.

Tancy located the knob on the lantern, turned out the light, and climbed into bed beside Jemmy. The murmuring ceased.

"Amen," said Miss Michaels.

The dormitory was officially at rest.

At Gaither's Mill, when Tancy went to bed, the night sounds came up, and she fell asleep listening to whippoorwills and pulsing locusts. Here were none of those reassuring sounds, but instead laughter and voices from the hotel saloon and people talking on the gallery and, for a long time, two drunken men quarreling under the dormitory windows. It didn't seem to bother Miss Michaels or the teacher. How could they sleep with a racket like that going on outside?

Furthermore, Tancy was not accustomed to a pillow or to a mattress, and the bedsprings threatened to pitch her right off every time she turned over. It was worse than riding that horse this morning.

Tancy wasn't feeling homesick exactly — yes, she was. Homesick was exactly how she was feeling. That chemical odor hurt her throat. What if it made her sick in this strange place, so far away from home? She missed the smells of home. She wished she could stay with Stud's family, in the jail. She wished (she had to admit it) she was back at Gaither's Mill, lying on her pallet beside Miss Puddin's bed.

"Tancy." Jemmy sighed in his sleep. She touched the nape of his neck, where his hair spiraled close and wiry looking, but really it was soft and fine, like fine silk, like petting a mouse. He lay in a hollow, and she was afraid of rolling on top of him and maybe smothering him to death.

When she figured that Miss Michaels had surely gone to sleep, she slipped out of bed and spread her blanket on the floor. There she could at least be comfortable, even if she couldn't sleep. The next she knew, Miss Michaels was kneeling by her side and the window frames behind her were black in the gray dawn light.

"What happened to you?" said Miss Michaels.

"I must have fallen out of the bed," said Tancy.

11

AFTER BREAKFAST, the teacher from the dormitory led a reluctant Jemmy off to her school, which had been set up in the kitchen of the former jail. They had trouble getting books and writing materials, Miss Michaels said; and as for the teachers, well – they came and went.

"We inherited this last one from Shantytown," she said. "Coming from there, she's already discouraged, so don't be surprised if you find yourself teaching school before too long."

Shantytown, Miss Michaels said, was just what it sounded like – a horrible little settlement of shacks on the outskirts of Knoxford, built by drifters too trifling or too naive to make contracts with their former masters.

Tancy loved everything about her new job. She loved her office. She loved the stool that Mr. Emory, the guard, brought for her to sit on behind the wooden table. She loved her new ledger, the inkwell, the clean cloth for wiping her pen nib when it clogged. She sat up straight on her stool, elegant in Miss Michaels's high-collared shirtwaist and the long navy skirt from Supply; and she tapped her penstaff on the table in a businesslike way and said, "Next, please." The morning went by so fast she was astonished when Miss Michaels said it was time for lunch. *Lunch,* said Tancy to herself.

"We're doing so well," said Miss Michaels, "I think I'll ask Mr. Emory to bring our platters to the office so we can work right through lunchtime."

Platters. Lunchtime. The stylish words spread through Tancy's mouth, like something savored. "Name, please, and state your need," she said, and looked into the face of a large-bosomed woman wearing a pink bonnet with green ribbon streamers. *Tancy's bonnet!*

"I declare!" said the woman. "Ain't you the gal that come into town with us yesterday? With your little baby brother?" She did not wait for an answer. "What you doing in here?"

"I got a job," Tancy managed to reply.

"I got *me* a bonnet." The woman cocked her head and posed. "Ain't this just about the prettiest bonnet you ever did see?"

Tancy felt sick. "Your name, please," she repeated.

"Witherspoon, honey," said the woman grandly. "Martha Washington Witherspoon."

*

By the time they closed the office that night and went out to the backyard for supper, Tancy felt almost as though she belonged. It came from knowing what to expect. The same cook stirred the hominy with his hoe; the same dishwashers passed out plates. Then Tancy caught sight of the pink bonnet across the yard and her well-being vanished. It wasn't fair. That bonnet was meant to be hers, just as soon as she had earned the money to pay for it.

At supper tonight, a little girl wore it. Her mother paraded her around the yard and showed her off.

"Look, Tancy!" Jemmy raced up, waving a battered slate. "I learnt to spell my name. Watch." He inscribed a ponderous *J* with a stub of chalk.

Stud followed Jemmy, diffident in the presence of Tancy, the office worker. "Can I talk to you once?"

The boy drew a line of splendid *J*'s. "Stud goes to my school. I'm smarter than him."

"Hush, Jemmy. You've been going to school, Stud?"

"I am smarter," Jemmy persisted. "Teacher gave me Stud's slate cause he writes so bad. He writes like this." Jemmy seized his chalk with a hammer grip.

"Hush, I said, Jemmy. Go ask the cook for some supper." Tancy sent him off and apologized for him. "Little boys . . . !"

"Well, Jemmy said the truth – that's the way I write," Stud admitted. "Writing's hard; reading too. It's took me more'n a month to learn it all."

His schooling was finished, Stud said; he had gone through the blue-backed speller, and it was time to head out again. The dispensary had pretty well cured their Muh's itch, and she was raring to go. "I been waiting all day to tell you," he said.

His words died between them. Tancy had located the bonnet again, this time perched on the head of a very tall woman. Stud followed her glance.

"There's the gal that cleans the jail, wearing the bonnet," he said. Glad – her name was Gladys – had been perishing to buy that bonnet from the day they put it in the window; but Glad was too grease-fingered, where it came to money, and spent all she made on candy. Put three bits in her hand and she didn't turn around twice before she tore off to the grocery store.

"Then how did she get the bonnet?" Tancy asked. "A Wither-spoon woman told me it belonged to her."

"Leave it to Glad," Stud said, laughing. He told how Glad had got the Witherspoon slaves to pool their pennies together with hers, on agreement that they would take turns wearing the bonnet. "She've been at her folks in the jail to go shares, but none of them had any money to speak of, and anyway, most of them gone back to Shufords' . . . hey, wait, where you going?"

But Tancy was already plucking at the tall woman's sleeve. "Gladys? You're Gladys from Shufords'?"

"I'm her." Gladys adjusted the green bow beneath her chin.

"From Elvira Shuford's?"

"Yes, girl. Widow Shuford. Mrs. Colonel Thad Shuford, that was."

Tancy clasped her hands prayerfully. "Do you know my mother at Shufords' – her name is Lulu. Sometimes they called her Lucy."

Gladys shook her head. "No Lulu at Shufords' that I know about, nor Lucy neither."

"Maybe they gave her a different name when they bought her. She came from Gaither's; it was a long time ago, over fifteen years ago; I was just a baby."

Gladys said coyly, "Honey, I been too young to remember fifteen years ago." But she had a thought. "The dishwashers come from Shufords'; you could ask them. One of them is real old; she might remember."

But the two dishwashers, when Tancy asked them, could recall no Lulu, no Lucy at Shufords'.

"Shufords bought her from Gaither's," Tancy urged. "Can't you think of anybody bought from Gaither's – if her real name was Louella, maybe, or Lucille?"

The older of the two women ruminated. She said slowly, "Lucinda . . . ?"

"Could have been a name like that," Tancy encouraged.

"Seems to me like they was a Lucinda from Gaither's – some woman that the Shufords got rid of right away – no, don't get your hopes up. I can't say for sure they was any Lucinda, honey. My membrance ain't what it used to be."

Think! Think! Tancy wanted to tell the woman.

Stud hovered at her elbow. "Us leaving tomorrow, Tancy, I thought we could talk."

Try to remember, Tancy silently pleaded, her eyes on the dishwasher.

"You like that bonnet, Tancy?" Stud asked eagerly. "I get you one like it. I know where they make them, in the military."

"*Millinery*," said Tancy, testily.

"I get you any color you want. Pink, like that one, or yellow. Blue. What color you like?"

"Not any color," said Tancy. "I wouldn't wear that show-off rig if you begged me to." She jerked her elbow from Stud's grasp and stalked off.

Lucinda definitely sounded like a clue Tancy ought to explore, Miss Michaels agreed that night, preparing for bed. "But why don't you wait a couple of weeks and ride the cargo wagon when it goes? It'll take you within a mile of the Shuford plantation."

Tancy thought of confronting the redoubtable Elvira and assented.

"And in the meantime, who knows, your mother might just turn up here, looking for you."

That sounded logical. All through the day Tancy had interviewed people looking for their families. Looking for food, looking for jobs, land — where should they apply for their forty acres? they wanted to know. Their mule?

Miss Michaels dragged off her mobcap and tied back the careless twist of her long brown hair. "The government actually did promise forty acres last year," she said, getting into bed. "Politics. It's criminal the way they've told that, and then turned the slaves loose, without any resources for making their own way, and nothing but a puny agency like this bureau to help them."

Tancy disagreed. "It helped me and Jemmy." She owed her job to the bureau! She was earning money, her first real pay, making her own living.

"I'm not talking about you, Tancy. You're different." Miss Michaels sat up in the bed. "But you see what some of them do, as soon as a little money comes into their hands. They rush right out and spend it in the most *ridiculous* way."

"Ridiculous," Tancy hastened to agree. Good thing she hadn't bought that bonnet!

Miss Michaels lay back down. "Don't listen to me," she said, "I'm just making conversation." She closed her eyes and crossed her arms over her chest.

Tancy climbed into the bed with Jemmy. She had discussed politics with Miss Michaels! She had contradicted her, defended her own position — a real conversation. And not once had she felt self-conscious about it! What a friend she had found in Miss Michaels.

"But I don't admire her mobcap," she breathed in Jemmy's ear.

"M-m-mn."

"I'd feel ridiculous wearing a thing like that," she told him. She shifted and bounced on the springy cot. It was an honor to sleep on a regular bed; she was determined to master it. But it sagged in the middle, and she kept rolling down on top of Jemmy.

"Um, um," he mumbled, snuggling up to her. His hand brushed her breast. Stroked her breast. His hand fondled her breast and his mouth made clicking sounds.

"Stop that!" she hissed, and slapped his hand.

Briefly, Jemmy opened blurred, astonished eyes. He sighed, and succumbed once more to slumber.

It was a sin to let a boy touch you. Miss Puddin said so. But Jemmy was only a little boy, and he was asleep; he didn't know he was doing something naughty.

Nasty, Miss Puddin had said, shaming Jemmy. Nasty, nasty. If Tancy ever had a little boy of her own, she would want him to be just like Jemmy, and she would never, ever, tell him he was nasty.

Tancy stroked one of the boy's knobby knees. It was going to be hard to give him up when they found his mother, she realized sadly. That could happen tomorrow. The roads were full of people trying to find their families, Miss Michaels said.

The dormitory was stifling. Tancy's long-sleeved nightgown (Miss Michaels's nightgown) felt thick and oppressive. Tancy slipped from the bed to look out the open window. She could hear laughter and the convivial clink of glasses in the hotel saloon. She thought of the tepid water in the dormitory bucket, and of the water barrel in the hallway downstairs, replenished twice a day with cold well water.

She crept down the narrow, steep steps, past the padlocked dispensary on the second floor, down the wider stairs to the ground floor. For a time she stood at the water barrel, in the stagnant darkness, and looked toward the back, where the glass-paned door let in a square of dull light. She walked the length of the hall to look out at the shadowy yard. On an impulse, she released the bolt, stepped outside, and raised her arms to the moon.

The stars shone but faintly in the heavy atmosphere. The young moon tilted softly within its nimbus – all poured out, Julia used to say; no more rain. They needed rain. It was already too late for salvaging the corn and tobacco, and if they didn't get some autumn rains, there'd be short rations next winter.

A movement along the fence distracted her. She looked closer and discerned a couple there, passionately embracing. For some reason the spectacle made her feel melancholy.

"What are you doing out here, Tancy?"

Stud! At once her mood lifted. "I came out to get cool for a minute," she said. "It was so hot upstairs." She added generously, "And I wanted to say good-bye, in case I missed you tomorrow. Tell your Muh I said good-bye."

"I do that." He answered her coolly.

"Heading to Salisbury, did you say?"

"Raleigh."

"Can they find your father for you in Raleigh?"

He thawed a little. Raleigh was the bureau headquarters. They didn't guarantee anything, but as his Muh said, what had the bureau done for them here in Knoxford?

Tancy got an idea. "Could you ask them about my mother in Raleigh, when you get there? Her name's Lucinda. Do you remember her? They called her Lulu, or Lucy sometimes."

"What she look like?"

Tancy couldn't tell him that. "She was Go-Charlie's mother too, Uncle Swamp said. Did you know Go-Charlie?"

He shook his head. "I'll ask Muh." His Muh had good remembrance, Stud bragged. Who was kin to who. When things happened. "Muh'll know, if anybody does. Us'll ask in Raleigh and get word to you, one way or another."

"Thank you, Stud. Do you know, you are so good! I'm really going to miss you."

Stud growled like somebody embarrassed.

Tancy took his arm and leaned a little against his shoulder. Stud *was* nice, like a brother to her.

By accident, perhaps, his hand brushed her breast.

"I have to go in," she said.

"Wait a little," Stud whispered. "We leaving early tomorrow. Now's the only time we got to talk." The hand brushed again, paused, and ever so stealthily, fondled her breast.

"Stop that!" She struck at him. "What makes you think you can touch me there?"

"I didn't mean —"

"Yes, you did! You think I don't know what you meant?"

"Well, you let Billy, in the smokehouse —" he began.

"I never let Billy nothing! You know how that was! You never did anything to help me either, just stood there looking on. *Looking on!* Nasty! I'm glad I wasn't born a man, all men ever think of is nasty." She marched up the steps.

"Don't go," Stud pleaded. "I won't — I promise I won't — and this is the last time we'll get to see each other —"

She went inside and shot the door bolt. She didn't care if she never saw him again, she was so disgusted.

To make matters worse, Miss Michaels was sitting up in her

bed when Tancy slipped back into the dormitory. "Did you lock the door when you came in?" she asked.

Tancy couldn't see her expression. "I went down to get a drink of cold water," she said.

Miss Michaels lay back without saying more. Tancy lay down too, and balanced on the edge of the mattress until she ached. Finally she gave up and made the blanket into a pallet on the floor, but it wasn't until long after the hotel saloon closed up that she slept.

12

As it turned out, Tancy never rode the cargo wagon to the Shuford plantation. Instead, the second week in August, Elvira Shuford came to the bureau in Knoxford, "to gather up my niggers," as she said.

The two women dishwashers submitted to their former mistress from old habit, and sat passively waiting in the carryall while Mrs. Shuford harangued Gladys out on the wooden sidewalk. Tancy, copying letters for Captain Dobbins, recognized the penetrating voice, and from the provost's window, she spied on the scene.

Tall Gladys, minus the pink bonnet, seemed visibly to dwindle as Mrs. Shuford preached to her about her mammy and pappy back at the plantation. And what about the Misses Dilly, Pleasant, Tempe, and Pru? Didn't Gladys care about *any* of her folks?

Tancy could see Gladys weakening. In another minute Mrs. Shuford would bundle her into the carryall with the others and head out of town. If Tancy was to speak to her now, she must not delay. She rushed from the office, out the front door and around the corner, and halted a respectful distance from the two women.

"Yes'm," Gladys was saying with downcast face. "Yes'm, I reckon you right. I'll go get my duds." She moved disspiritedly toward the backyard.

"Excuse me, Miss Elvira," said Tancy, and stopped, tongue-tied. Her heart pounded. She felt weak. She was not going to be able to speak.

"What you want?" said Mrs. Shuford. "Do I know you from somewheres? Whose nigger are you?"

Nobody's! Tancy wanted to yell at her. She straightened and opened her mouth.

"Say, ain't you Cornelia Gaither's gal? I thought I knowed you from somewheres! What you want?"

"My mother," said Tancy, her voice mercifully returning. With an effort she raised her eyes.

"Law, girl, I ain't got your mammy that I know of. What's your mammy's name? Listen!" she exclaimed. "What you doing here in this town anyway? You better get back to Gaither's, where you belong."

"I've got a job here," said Tancy. "Miss Elvira — "

"You've got a job at Gaither's Mill, and that's where you'd ought to be, right this very minute, your missus back there working her fingers to the bone and nobody to help her. Oh," she said cunningly, "if you saw how lonesome she is without you. Cries all the day long."

Tancy felt a wrench. Miss Puddin crying for her? That hurt. But she stood her ground. "She was lonesome for you too, Miss Elvira, when you didn't call after Billy died."

Mrs. Shuford didn't seem to notice this impudence. "Girl, back then, I couldn't go nowhere, with my niggers leaving in droves and nobody left to do the planting but just me and my girls." She added parenthetically, "I should've saved my seed, with this drought. But what's all this about your mammy?"

Lucinda, said Tancy. Called Lulu by Mas Gaither, and Lucy by Julia. Did Mrs. Shuford remember if the colonel ever bought a woman named Lucinda from Mas Gaither?

Mrs. Shuford took a long time answering.

Lucinda. She drawled the name out and narrowed her eyes. Oh yes, she remembered the colonel buying Lulu, she certainly did. And sold her within the week, no loss to anybody; sold her for the same reason Will Gaither had to. "Lulu was a bad woman, girl; you probably know what I mean. You're lucky you had a good woman like your missus to raise you up, stead of Lulu."

Tancy said, in a small voice, "Who did he sell her to?"

"Why, to nobody! Colonel wouldn't sell that kind of a woman to anybody he thought anything of. Some speculator took her off his hands, and you know what that means — the chain gang. She been run south in a wagon, to work rice in Louisiana or Mississippi or some such. No telling what's come of her — dead, likely; they don't last too long down there."

Gladys came out of the backyard, hurrying this time, with many a sly glance behind her. She carried something tied in a cloth that she handled with great care, and she scrambled into the back seat of the carryall with the other two women. One of them snatched Gladys's bundle with a smothered laugh, and Tancy caught a glimpse of pink.

Mrs. Shuford said, with immense kindliness, "Now, why don't you come on back with me, girl? I'll drop you off at Gaither's and garntee you won't be sorry you went. You niggers ain't never going to make a go of it on your own, and it's all different now, see, you work on shares or for pay. I went out and rounded up all my folks to come back and work on shares. They'll thank me for it, harvesttime."

To her mortification, Tancy found herself nodding.

Mrs. Shuford said, "You'll thank me too, you'll see. Your missus been a real mother to you. I know you don't want to sorrow your mother. You come jump in the carryall and go back with us, do."

It would have been so easy to say yes. It was always hard to say no to a white person. But Tancy was learning. She said blandly, "Some other time, Miss Elvira. I can't come right now."

Miss Michaels, when she told her, said Lucinda might still show up "someday," but her tone said "not likely." Tancy thought it unlikely too. At least she and Jemmy still had each other.

*

The schoolteacher quit before August was over, just as Miss Michaels had predicted. Tancy took her place in the classroom, flattered by the assignment; but what she found there disheartened her. She hunted up Miss Michaels and found her in conference with the provost marshall.

"There aren't enough slates to go around," she reported.

"I know," said Miss Michaels, with a glance that rebuked the provost.

"And I've got five pupils who have to share one desk!"

"I know."

"Can we at least buy some more books?"

"No!" said Captain Dobbins. "We're not trying to run a fancy academy here. I said so at the beginning, and I'll not authorize any more army money for it."

"You've spent so much on the school already," said Miss Michaels, "and the bureau's other programs are proving so successful."

The captain raised a weary hand. "Save your sarcasm for the next provost," he advised her.

"The next provost! Dare I hope?"

"Good luck to the both of us, Miss Michaels."

Tancy, bewildered, tiptoed from the room. She had gone there merely to report a shortage. Whatever did she say to stir up such an exchange? She returned to the classroom and worked out a schedule for rotating the books and writing materials among the students.

But in a way, Tancy understood the captain's objections to the school. Her pupils were of all ages, and the enrollment fluctuated daily, sometimes drastically, as whole families dropped in and out of the school. The discipline of youngsters whose parents were also her students made her nervous. The discipline of students too old to be bossed made her nervous. So, when a young minister from Massachusetts appeared at the bureau one day, on a stated mission of redemption for Southern whites as well as Southern blacks, she gladly surrendered her two weeks' teaching tenure in exchange for a position in the complaints office.

Captain Dobbins placed the high-minded minister in the schoolroom and said he could preach there on Sundays to all who cared to come. A fair number of his pupils attended his services, but not a single white townsman. In fact, the hapless cleric could not find a boarding house in the town that would take him in. Captain Dobbins finally agreed to let him sleep at the barracks down at the railroad station and eat his meals in the yard.

All through September Tancy wrote up grievances for the provost to rule on. The family quarrels and petty disputes brought to the bureau sounded like the arguments that Mas Gaither used to settle on the spot, back at Gaither's Mill. But in October the charges grew more serious, following a poor harvest. Sharecroppers began accusing their employers of cheating on the division of crops and of withholding wages.

Tancy wearied of reminding the unhappy tenants, "No matter what the contract promises, if the planter doesn't make any crop, he doesn't make any money, and if he doesn't make any money, he can't pay you. Half of nothing is nothing," she kept telling her irate clients.

"The people over in Shantytown keep them stirred up," Miss

Michaels said. She disapproved of the shabby settlements of blacks that had sprung up over the state since the war's end. The people who lived in them were troublemakers, she said. They blamed the bureau for not helping them, when they themselves refused to work for their former masters. She had no patience whatsoever with such malcontents, Miss Michaels said.

Tancy, forgetting her own impatience, defended the malcontents. "That's because you don't know what it's like to be a slave."

Miss Michaels blinked. "No, I don't," she conceded. "But you have to admit that those tin shacks in Shantytown are worse than slave cabins ever were."

Tancy had never seen the tin shacks of Shantytown. Still she felt qualified to argue. "At least the shacks belong to *them*."

*

During the weeks of her employment, Tancy had kept her wages in a kind of cloth pocket that she pinned under her waistband. At night she and Jemmy counted the handful of silver together. "Just think, Jemmy, one of these will buy a whole acre of land." She laid a silver dollar in his hand.

"How much candy?"

She gloated over the hoard, and longed for Jemmy to share her dreams of ownership. "For this many dollars, we could buy fifteen acres of land. We could have us a little farm, like Miss Puddin's, only littler. Remember Miss Puddin?"

"No. I want candy."

Chaps forgot so quickly! Jemmy no longer talked about finding his mother. Just as well.

The secret pocket fattened. On the advice of Miss Michaels, Tancy deposited her dollars in the Freedmen's Branch Bank in Knoxford, retaining only a few half-dimes in the pocket for emergencies.

"I think you're wise. The bank will pay you interest, and it's a good way to save," said Miss Michaels. "Also, you oughtn't to carry large sums of money on your person. Some of these people coming into the bureau look like they'd cut your throat for a dollar."

The character of the applicants had changed; Tancy saw that. Hard times and a prolonged cold spell made them desperate. Winter lay ahead. They wanted their forty acres right now, and they obviously didn't believe her when she told them the bureau had no land to dispense. They complained that the midwife who doled out the medicine wasn't a real doctor. They wanted more food. In December a woman student barged into her office calling for dismissal of the missionary.

"He wants to preach at us, not teach us," she said. "Over in Shantytown, they got a *real* teacher. The chillun got they own book and they own slate, and they ain't none of it broke or tore up neither."

When Tancy tried to explain the provost's decree, the woman began shouting and demanding first his dismissal and then Tancy's. Where were these obnoxious people coming from anyway?

"They're restless," said Miss Michaels. "You know it's going to be a terrible Christmas for them. With worse times ahead. My guess is they'll close the bureau down after New Year's.'

Miss Michaels shrugged at Tancy's shocked face. "The bureau was chartered for only one year. There's a bill in Congress to appropriate funds for extending it, but you know a president like Andrew Johnson would veto it, even if it passed. Oh yes, my dear. It wouldn't hurt to start looking for another job right now."

Tancy was stunned. Her job was at stake – her life! The bureau really was her life; she felt comfortable here, she had worked at one time or another in every office in the place. She felt thankful now to have saved her money; she was going to need it.

On a slack afternoon close to Christmas, Tancy and Jemmy walked along the main street and looked in all the store windows. The glut of material goods for sale never failed to astound her. Jemmy moved far easier in this cosmopolitan world than she did.

Already the bolts of cloth and laces at the mantua maker's bored him; to him the curlicue throne inside the barber's palace was nothing but another chair.

"Look at that great big saw, Jemmy," she urged him, outside the hardware store. Any boy ought to be fascinated by tools. "You could cut down the biggest tree in the world with that saw."

"I know it." Blasé Jemmy tugged her on to the grocery store, where a glass case at the cash counter displayed Christmas candies. There were candy canes striped like the barber's pole, scrolls of sugar ribbon, taffies, gelatins, and rows of gorgeous chocolates in fluted paper. "Buy me candy," he implored her, jigging with desire. "Please! I want it, Tancy, really and truly I do!"

"I can't buy you candy." She hurried him out of the store. "I don't have any money."

"You do have money, Tancy! You have it under your dress — here, I'll show you." He yanked up her skirt, right there on the street, where people all around could see.

"Stop that!" She slapped his hand. "You nasty boy! I'm never going to buy you candy, you acting nasty like that."

Jemmy's mouth dropped open.

Strong arms encircled her from behind and squeezed her hard. "Tancy, sugar! You still here! I'uz scared you be gone from this place, time we got back." It was Stud, large and solid and comforting.

The unexpected reunion flustered her. Right there in the street with her skirt pulled up! "It's nice to see you again," she muttered.

The weeks in Raleigh had made of Stud a city man, with smartly barbered hair and a natty mustache, a confident air. "They told me at the bureau you was in the town someplace."

Jemmy just stood there with his mouth hanging open, looking simple. Tancy said to him, "You remember who this is, don't you?"

Jemmy hung his head. "Stud," he said, in a shy, little-boy voice.

"Well, can't you say hey to him? Stud's our friend, from back home."

Jemmy stuck out his lower lip and scuffed at the ground. She wanted to smack him!

They started back to the bureau, where Stud said his family was planning to spend the night. "You get the letter I written you from Raleigh?" he asked.

Tancy shook her head. "What did you say in it?"

"How us-all ask in Raleigh and everywhere along the road, but ain't nobody know where your mammy gone to."

"Where my – oh!" She had not thought of Lucinda in weeks. She felt obscurely guilty and ashamed, and she asked quickly, "How about your daddy, did you locate him?"

"Not in Raleigh, but they say he gone to Gaither's hunting us. I written him a letter to wait for us there. Written you a letter and written one to pappy." Then he confessed, "Took me two whole days to do it. I ruther dig ditches with the ground froze than do writing."

"Writing's easy!" cried Jemmy, himself once more.

"But they wan't any way out of it," Stud continued earnestly. "We had to let Pappy know we was on the way, so's he won't strike out again fore we get there."

"I can write, I can write good, can't I, Tancy?" the little boy persisted. "I can write faster than anybody, if I want to, can't I, Tancy?"

At last Stud noticed the child. "Jemmy." He snapped his fingers. "I purely forgot to tell you about Jemmy's ma. We found *her*! Anyways, Muh found out where she is. They was this old woman in Raleigh, see, that Muh got to talking to, said she knowed a woman from Gaither's, the old woman did, and asking about this one and that one, and by-and-by Muh figured out it was Mary she was talking about. Now, what do you think of that?"

Stud told his news again, for the triumph of it. Shantytown right outside Knoxford! Not much farther from the bureau than you'd stretch the truth, if you were given to lying. "Us got your mammy for you, son!" he told Jemmy joyfully.

Jemmy took stealthy hold of Tancy's skirt.

"You gonna see your mammy this very day!"

"Shantytown?" said Tancy faintly.

"Or Ragtown or Slabtown or Boxtown, however they name it. We seen one they called Tin Cup on our way to Raleigh, a bunch of shanties made out of old pieces of tin. The white folks from in town come there for somebody to carpenter for them or fix them up some herb medicine or do day work. Yeh. Shantytown."

"Mary's in Shantytown — you're sure it's Jemmy's mother? A name like Mary, that could be anybody's mother."

"No, it's her. She been all over looking for the boy — Gaither's and all over. Muh talked to that old woman a long whiles." Stud was positive. "Muh got good remembrance, I told you. I'll carry the boy to Shantytown for you," he offered helpfully. "We staying in the jail so we ain't have to camp out, take us all tomorrow to get to Gaither's. I got time to run Jemmy to Shantytown and still get back for supper."

"No!" Jemmy screamed suddenly. He grabbed Tancy around the knees. "I don't want to! Don't let him, Tancy!"

"What you hollering about, boy? Don't want to go to your own mammy? Shame on you!" Stud seized the child sternly.

"Hush, Stud. I'll handle this," Tancy said. "You go on out back. I'll see you at suppertime." She hustled Jemmy into the bureau and upstairs. In the safety of the dormitory, they stood and stared at one another for a long frightened moment. But what were they afraid of?

She read to him for a while. The clinking and chatter from down in the backyand depressed her, and she began singing all the songs she could remember, to cheer herself up. She taught Jemmy the rain song. She helped him work the chain puzzle Mr. Emory had made him out of three shiny links. They played the dot game on Jemmy's slate until it got too dark to see the dots. Then she lit the coal-oil lantern and they sat together on his bed. Ever since the first schoolteacher went home to Connecticut, he had had a bed to himself.

The ghost of Mary hovered in the silence between them, but neither mentioned her name.

"I want my supper," Jemmy said at last, uneasily.

She cupped his face in her hands and stroked his satiny cheeks with her thumbs. How could she give this boy up? She loved everything about him, his energetic body, the sweet nape of his neck where the hair whorled into a line of soft beads, his impish eyes, lustrous now in the lantern light. She could never resist pat-pat-patting that springy little behind of his.

"Supper," he said again, through lips pinched into a pout by her hands. She had to kiss that plump pouting mouth.

"Tancy'll go bring Jemmy some supper," she said. "You wait here for me."

"My go wiss you." Whenever Jemmy was frightened or upset, he reverted to baby talk.

"Down where Stud is? That's where I'm going. You want to go see Stud?" She fixed him with her eyes: Stud will carry you to Shantytown, her eyes warned him.

He regarded her with alarm. She despised herself for threatening him. "Lie down, if you don't feel good, honey," she suggested, and she tempted him. "Nobody is allowed up here except Tancy and Miss Michaels. Tancy'll go bring you something to eat and stay up here with you, *if you don't feel good.*"

Jemmy's eyes gleamed. He turned painfully on the bed. "My's sick," he agreed, in a conspiratorial whisper.

Fire had gone out under the iron pot in the backyard, but there remained a residue of the meal congealing at the pit of its round belly. Tancy scraped a gob of greens and turnips into a tin cup. The moon shone full, benevolent, a Christmas moon. A sharp wind made her shiver. The crisp night had driven indoors everybody except Stud. He had waited in the yard for her.

"I had to put Jemmy to bed," she told him. "Too much excitement, probably. He was just a baby when Mary was sold off."

Stud nodded indifferently. "I like to talk to you, Tancy. See, we be gone in the morning, before you wake up, maybe, so they won't be no time then." He had to follow her back to the steps. "So you got to decide right now and get ready if you coming with us, cause Muh ain't waiting on you nor nobody else in the morning."

"Coming with your Muh — what are you talking about?"

"Not coming with Muh. With me. Back to Gaither's." In the moonlight, Stud's cheekbones shone with the effort of declaring his intentions. She saw him braid his fingers. "If we was to go back . . . together, see . . . I'll get my own place, big enough for me and for you too. *You* know."

"I don't," said Tancy, although she suspected she did. "What has you going back to Gaither's got to do with me?"

They could go back to their old jobs, he explained — Stud running the mill the way he used to and Tancy waiting on Mrs. Gaither, except now they would both be drawing wages; and with the two of them bringing money in, they could save up to buy their own place, own their own property. They were allowed to do that now. Land was cheap, dollar an acre, he heard.

She felt suddenly released. His braiding hands gave her confidence. "What makes you think Mrs. Gaither will take you back?" she inquired, out of a lovely calm.

"Cause I know how to run that mill." Stud answered strongly. He moved on sure ground now. "And mistis, she knows I know how."

"She knows you cut out of there when she needed you," Tancy reminded him. "You think she's forgotten about that?"

Stud's eyes glinted in the moonlight. "Gaither's ain't the only mill I know how to run!"

And running a mill wasn't the only thing he could do, he wanted her to know. Many was the job he'd done on the long road to Raleigh and back, blacksmithing in one place, coopering in another, a stretch on the railroad when they'd hit Greensboro — his Muh and the chaps never missed a meal, the entire time they'd been looking for their pappy. "Boss man beg me to stay, every time we move on," Stud bragged. "Folks that has to pay out money in these times knows a good hand when they see it. Dollar a day and glad to pay."

Indeed, Tancy believed him. Stud had always been a reliable fellow, and working and traveling about the state had given him a fine air of assurance. He was a different man. With his head flung back and powerful shoulders riding easily on that sturdy frame, even her critical eye acknowledged him a "good hand." Still she could not resist baiting him.

"If you're worth a dollar a day, how come you're going back to Gaither's? You aren't going to get any dollar a day there, not from Miss Puddin, you aren't."

His Muh still hadn't rounded up their set, he explained patiently, and he was the only one of her chaps big enough to help until they were reunited with Pappy.

Tancy sniffed. "You've got a brother as old as I am. He ought to be big enough to see your mama back to Gaither's, now that you know your daddy's there."

Stud hunched his shoulders. "Muh got it in her head for us chaps to stay by her and Pappy," he admitted. "Us been scattered around for so long."

Tancy had never cared for bossy Alberta, the mother of that close family. She said sweetly, "And your mama's got you on a string."

"It ain't exactly that, Tancy," the man pleaded. "See, I been thinking how it used to was, back on the old range, and wanting to go back there. It's a pretty place. We growed up there. We had good times there. You remember how we carried old Mas in his chair clear around the house at the barn raising? And how he just laughed about it and brought out a bucket of brandy and give everybody all they could drink, and a big supper after they got up the barn? You could sit around and eat and drink till you almost bust."

"Fellows could," said Tancy. "The women got to do the cooking and had to clean up afterward."

"Y'all ate too!"

"After the men got finished."

"Well, the fire, and the games and the dancing was for everybody."

"Not for me. Miss Puddin never let me do any of that."

"But it would be different if you went back there now! She'd have to let you, if we was m-m-mmarried." The word was out. Stud kicked at the step.

Tancy snickered, swift to take advantage. "Married! Whatever gave you the idea I wanted to get married?"

There was a long silence. At last, "Nothing," he admitted. "It's me that wants it. I'm asking you to."

His manliness shamed her. A flash of insight exposed her words to her for what they were: a deliberate cruelty, to punish him for finding Jemmy's mother. There was no such meanness in Stud, she knew that. Why did she want to hurt him? "Thank you," she said, with as much courtesy as she could manage. "I'm sorry, I can't do that." She ran up the back steps.

Stud leaped after her. "Wait, Tancy! You don't have to say right now —"

"I have to take care of Jemmy. He's sick."

"Get Mary to do that. She's his mammy, not you. I'll go fetch her here, if you want, and she can take over, and you and me can talk."

"No, Stud."

"Why not? Answer me, Tancy. Why won't you?" He almost wailed.

"Because I don't want to."

He followed her through the back door and along the hall, but he dared not pursue her up to the dormitory.

131

When she went downstairs the next morning, she learned that Stud and his family had departed. Before the sun came up, they told her in the backyard. Gone back to Gaither's; back to the old range.

Safe! was her first thought. Jemmy was still hers.

13

ON THEIR WALK that afternoon, Tancy took Jemmy to the grocery store and bought him a huge paper pokeful of candy.

The grocer didn't like trading with the blacks who had begun coming into his store, but Tancy guessed he liked even less turning down hard cash in these hard times. He indicated that she should deposit her money on the counter where he could retrieve it without touching her hand, and with a stony face he placed there the purchase for her to pick up. Still, he was a fair man. He filled the poke with as good a dime's worth as he would have given any white woman, and he did go to the further trouble of selecting a rainbow mixture of sweets.

Jemmy ate the whole pokeful before suppertime. The unaccustomed richness upset his stomach, and Tancy crouched beside him as he moaned in his sleep that night. Later, after midnight, he awoke and cried out in pain.

Miss Michaels rose from her bed and lit the lantern. "I just hope this is going to be a lesson to you both," she snapped. She swished across to the water bucket.

"My hurt, Tancy," Jemmy grieved, in a frail voice that wrung her heart.

"I know you do, honey. Tancy's so sorry."

"My don't want to hurt." Tears trickled from beneath his eyelids.

She kissed his eyelids, she wiped away his tears. "I would be sick in your place, if I could, darling."

"Firsty. My want some water."

Miss Michaels handed Tancy the dipper and went back to bed.

Tancy moistened a cloth to sponge the little boy's face. "Here. Don't drink it all at once."

He seized the dipper and began gulping.

"Not too fast, honey. It isn't good for you."

He thrust the dipper back in her hands. "More!"

His sick, pleading eyes forced her to bring him a second dipperful. He took two sips and paused.

"That's right, not so fast this time," she encouraged him.

He started to say something, but his words drowned in a flood of vomit that poured from his mouth, a vile river of undigested peas and pork swirling in viscous pink and yellow and green. The noxious mess soaked his nightshirt and spilled onto the bed. Tancy snatched him up in the sheet and rushed him to the chamberpot.

"Try to throw it up, honey," she whispered, supporting his retching, wretched body. "Get rid of it, you'll feel better." That was what Julia had told her the one time in her life that she had been sick and had to be doctored.

Jemmy was limp and half asleep by the time she got him cleaned up and into a fresh nightshirt. She had to carry him back to bed, where he lay so inert that she put her ear against his lips to make sure he was breathing. But his forehead felt cooler, he slept sweetly, and his lean little belly was soft to her touch.

Too much candy. Tancy had learned a lesson; Miss Michaels

didn't have to say it. What if it hadn't been too much candy? What if instead it had been something dreadful, like the summer complaint that wrung the life from a baby boy in the bureau jail during Tancy's first week in town? One day he laughed and staggered bowlegged in the backyard. Three days later he was a shrunken little old man with papery skin pleated on his arms, and the day after that he died.

What if something like that happened to Jemmy? Now she understood how the mother of that baby felt, that screaming mother. Now she knew how Miss Puddin felt, another screaming mother, the day they brought Billy home from the war.

She crept into bed beside Jemmy and closed her arms around him with utmost softness, so as not to disturb his slumber. She thought how she would be always careful with him hereafter, and train him to be careful as well, so that somehow he would be protected from all the troubles of the world; and because of her care, sorrow and pain and sickness should never touch him.

*

For Christmas Miss Michaels gave Jemmy a beautiful illustrated copy of *Seven Little Sisters*, ordered especially from New York. Tancy gave him *Original Poems for Infant Minds*, which she bought from the stationer's at a cost of one full week's wages. But it was Mr. Emory's gift of a homemade wooden top that Jemmy adored and suffered over. Mr. Emory could make a spinning top climb a ramp! Why couldn't Jemmy do the same?

"Play with something else," Tancy urged. "You could read one of your new books."

"They're *girl* books." He dealt *Seven Little Sisters* a scornful thump.

"There's a big boy's picture in the poem book." She showed him Greedy Richard, read aloud to him the poem about Dirty Jim; and the mother poem that must surely wring his heart, as it had hers:

When pain and sickness made me cry,
Who gazed upon my heavy eye
And wept for fear that I should die?
                        My mother.

And when I see thee hang thy head,
'Twill be my turn to watch thy bed,
And tears of sweet affection shed,
                        My mother.

The tremor in her voice moved him not at all. "I ain't gonna read no girl books."

"I *am not going to* read *any* girl books,' she corrected him

"Me neither," said Jemmy serenely. "Mr. Emory, he don't read no books atall."

Tancy said in a fury, "Mr. Emory is illiterate!"

"What's illiterate?"

She didn't want that getting back to Mr. Emory. "Mr. Emory is very clever with his hands," she amended.

It was a windy winter, and Mr. Emory had begun teaching Jemmy to build the perfect kite, so the books went under his folded nightshirt, in the crate beside his bed.

*

Spring came on early, bringing with it good rains and reviving hopes for the new growing season. The bureau heard fewer calls for forty acres and more for contracts with guarantees.

"At last they're showing some sense," Miss Michaels said. She had held all along that monitored sharecropping was the best way to make the new citizens independent.

Tancy wasn't sure she agreed. Here in April she still told a lot of the people, "Half of nothing is nothing."

Captain Dobbins declared a holiday on the anniversary of the war's end, and closed their offices for the day. In Knoxford stores stayed open for business as usual, and black crepe hung in their windows. Tancy, seeing the crepe, dreamed that night, as she had before, of Billy Gaither coming home from the war. In her dream the mother screaming was not always Miss Puddin. Sometimes it was Mary. Screaming dreadfully. Screaming and pleading and crying.

It was a punishment dream, she knew that – the price she had to pay for Jemmy. She had postponed from week to week any trip to Shantytown. Definitely she would take him there, she told herself, when the bureau job ran out.

In June she applied for a job at the Freedmen's Branch Bank and was offered wages equal to those at the bureau, except that she would have to find her own food and lodging. Miss Michaels advised her to hold off until Congress determined the fate of the bureau.

14

TO NO ONE'S surprise, President Johnson vetoed a bill that extended their operation for another year; but in midsummer, unexpectedly, Congress overrode the presidential veto and appropriated money for the bureau to work with.

Captain Dobbins fumed—he had counted on a transfer to California when the Knoxford office closed—and for once Miss Michaels commiserated with him; she too wanted the captain transferred to California. Or anywhere else.

"At least your job is safe now," she told Tancy. "You'd have hated working in the bank."

"Oh, yes...." said Tancy.

But she had grown tired of the cranky, demanding people who passed through the complaints office. Tired also of the inflexible army procedures she had once executed with such competence and pride.

And the paperwork! The duplicate invoices, the duplicate requisitions, the duplicate receipts. She wrote letters and copies of letters, and kept separate records of letters sent and received. She wrote out Captain Dobbins's reports for him, and made copies of the reports—no wonder the man longed for California!

So she was glad enough when the disillusioned young missionary gave up and went back to Massachusetts, and Captain Dobbins appointed her permanently to the schoolroom.

The equipment had not improved in her absence. Her students were the same unwieldy mix of old and young as before, with the added burden of Jemmy, who constantly disrupted the classroom, vying for her attention.

"He gets jealous when he sees you working with other children," Miss Michaels said. "I wouldn't worry about it. It's just a stage."

They sat on their beds in the breathless attic dormitory, talking the problem out, after their usual custom, while they fanned themselves. This summer, Miss Michaels herself seemed to be going through a stage. The bureau's extended operation had pleased her, but she too felt vaguely dissatisfied. "I wish I'd gone home for a visit at Christmas. When Mother hears that I'm not coming home at all —"

"What will she do?"

"Oh, the usual. She'll throw a tantrum, she'll get sick, she'll write me sweet, forgiving letters so I'll know what pain I'm causing her — Why?" she demanded of Tancy. "Why do women do this to each other?"

"I don't know," said Tancy, shaking her head. Perhaps mothers went through stages too. Miss Puddin had, after Billy died. People did change, they forgot. Children got over being homesick; Jemmy never mentioned his mother, for example, and as for Tancy — I haven't thought about Lulu in ages! she realized.

*

With deliberate malice, it seemed, summer rains bypassed piedmont North Carolina. The early-plowed fields baked to clods in the kiln of June's sun. The spring-burgeoning corn withered and browned before it could tassel. If we don't get some rain soon, farmers repeated monotonously all through July; if it doesn't rain by August . . .

It was the same old story, but this year the freedmen chose to end it differently. Why wait around to be told again, "Half of nothing is nothing"? Before harvesttime, the bureau jail overflowed with sharecroppers on their way to somewhere else, to the sea islands where they heard land was cheap, to the south and west where they heard food was plentiful.

"They got fritter trees growing in Arkansas beside a molasses pond. Shake the tree and fritters fall in the pond," some said. "There's hogs walking round with forks sticking in they backs, begging somebody to eat them," others declared.

Agents looking for cheap labor came around to the bureau and carted off the gullible ones by the wagonload to Mississippi, where they said money grew on bushes. Miss Michaels fought a daily battle with Captain Dobbins for allowing it.

"They're exploiting these poor people, Captain," she accused him, "and you're letting them do it!"

The captain said, "Are they better off fulfilling those contracts you saddled them with, that leave them in debt to Old Massa?"

"Sir, you surely don't hold me responsible for the drought, two years in a row!"

The agents gave the blacks free transportation, he mentioned, and free food on the road — big savings for the bureau.

"Which savings I have no doubt you'll divert to the schoolroom!"

The captain merely smiled.

At night, now, when Miss Michaels said amen to her prayers, she added aloud, "God grant me forgiveness of Captain Dobbins."

At night, now, Tancy stayed late in the schoolroom, tutoring, trying to cram ABC's into her students before they moved on. She worked compulsively. This might be their last chance at formal education.

Jemmy, deprived of her company, turned aggressive. He yelled at Miss Michaels, and would not let her put him to bed. He fought with other boys out in the yard. When Tancy loaned

Seven Little Sisters to Melba Pruitt, her best pupil, he threw a tantrum.

"You said yourself it was a girl's book," Tancy reminded him.

"It's *my* book."

"I only loaned it to her. You weren't reading it."

"You like her better than you like me. You like her cause she's a good reader."

There was no denying it: Tancy did like a good reader; reading was important, and she had to help Melba read as much as she could while she could. But she certainly didn't love Melba more than she did Jemmy. "You're my little boy," she explained. "Melba's got her own mama to love her."

He looked unconvinced. Later on, when she bent over his bed to kiss him good night, he said, "Tell me about my mammy, my real mammy in Shantytown."

Tancy was startled. She was so sure he had forgotten! She hesitated. "You mean what Stud said, I suppose – "

"Not what Stud said, what you said," the boy persisted. "About my mammy, mama, *you* know." He rocked in the bed with his thumb at the ready and reminded her in a singsong, "About the road, and about how I feel my mama's feetprints."

Tancy winced. "That was a long time ago, when you were just a little chap, we don't remember about that."

"Yes, we do too remember it. Tell it, Tancy." He was getting worked up.

"It was a long time ago," she said grudgingly. "Your mama went off with the trader one day. So after you got older, you came up to the big house with me, and then I started taking care of you."

"No!" Jemmy twisted angrily. "Not like that. Tell it the way you *did*."

He wouldn't let her leave out anything, not the smallest detail. She had to tell about the trader's team of mules and the wagon with the board across where the driver sat. She had to hold out both arms to show how Mary reached for Jemmy, left standing in the lane, and how she called to him, screamed for him, until the wagon rolled out of sight. And then Jemmy squatted beside Mary's footprints in the soft dust. . . .

"Till it got dark," he prompted.

"For a while anyway."

"Till it got *dark*."

"All right, till it got dark. And then you went on back to the quarters."

Jemmy whimpered.

After he had fallen asleep, nursing his satisfaction and grief, she faced up at last to what she must do.

Miss Michaels came up to the dormitory in a savage mood. Today's transport wagon to Mississippi enraged her, as had last week's to Texas, and the one before to Arkansas. Some agents, she had heard, were making their naive passengers pay for passage to the promised land. And there was nothing she could do about it! The money appropriated by Congress for the benefit of freedmen was going instead to army personnel, for operating the bureau.

"We're getting five new officers tomorrow," she said bitterly, "to shuffle the people around so they won't know they've been cheated. How can the merciful Lord let this happen?"

She turned out the lantern and went to bed. For a while there was silence, and Tancy waited respectfully for her to finish her devotions. In the dark, Miss Michaels spoke out fervently, "Sir, I hope you rot in hell."

Was she addressing God, Tancy wondered, or Captain Dobbins?

She lay awake through the night, planning, and yet there wasn't much to plan. In the gray dawn light next morning she waited for Miss Michaels to dress and watched her hurry out of the dormitory. Then she rose, heavyheaded and heavyhearted, to prepare for the journey.

She washed in the basin behind the screen. She dressed in the shirtwaist Miss Michaels had given her, and inside the band of her graceful gored skirt, she pinned her money pocket. She made her bed. She folded Jemmy's clothes into a tight bundle; and when nothing remained to be done, she woke the boy and dressed him in his best kneepants and shirt and led him downstairs to wait outside while she spoke to Miss Michaels.

She could not bring herself to tell the woman she was taking Jemmy to Shantytown, to his mother. She felt too drained, too defeated to explain. Also, she was in no mood for one of Miss Michaels's lectures. She was giving Jemmy back to his mother; wasn't that more than enough?

"I have an appointment today at the Freedmen's Branch Bank, to discuss that job," she said, in a high, false voice. "You remember the job, that they said —"

Miss Michaels looked surprised. "Isn't it awfully early in the day for an appointment?" She answered her own question. "But of course; you've arranged to get back in time for school."

Tancy hung her head. She hadn't even thought about school. "I forgot."

"Dear girl, if you can't take responsibility for the job you have now, how can you expect —" Miss Michaels paused and expelled a breath. "Never mind. Go on. Take all the time you need, take the day off, why don't you? They've got all these military people coming in to run the bureau, let them worry about the school." She resumed checking a long list against her ledger.

Tancy regarded her friend sadly. The careless thrust of an escaped tendril of brown hair into the sensible mobcap, the proper poise of her penstaff, made Tancy want to cry.

Miss Michaels looked up. "Is something wrong?"

"No, nothing. I'll be going then. I thought I'd take Jemmy with me."

"You are right to do so. A prospective employer needs to understand that you have a young dependent. Good luck to you." Miss Michaels went back to her checking.

"Thank you." In a daze she backed out of the office. On the front stoop she took Jemmy's bundle in one hand and Jemmy's hand in the other, and together they started out.

Jemmy stumbled along, still drowsy. "Where are we going, Tancy?"

"Eat your breakfast," she snapped. The cook had given him a bacon rind to gnaw on.

The town was just beginning to come to life. A small barefoot boy scuffed down the center of the powdery street. With a towel the barber flapped dust from his striped pole. The saloon keeper propped wide his swinging half doors and flung handfuls of wet sawdust to cushion the approach of the thirsty. Business was slow in Knoxford; the long drought had dried up profits along with the crops, but shops opened every day as usual, to compete for whatever pennies were available.

Tancy and Jemmy walked the full length of Main Street, Jemmy chewing halfheartedly on his bacon rind. When they passed the last of the shops and walked through hilly residential streets, he looked around with interest at the new territory. "Where are we going, Tancy?" He yanked at her skirt. "Tancy?"

"Shantytown," she mumbled.

"Where Stud said my mama is?"

"Maybe." But she couldn't put it off any longer; she had to prepare him for the unknown. So she forced herself to tell him everything she knew about Mary, how pretty she was, with a pretty pointy chin and dimples when she smiled, and how she had hair long enough to comb to the top of her head, where she twisted it into a sleek, small loaf, like tangle-dough biscuit. "Jemmy was Mary's baby, her only-only baby, so you know she loved Jemmy more than anybody else in the world," said Tancy.

"More than Tancy?" Jemmy was pleased but greedy.

She dropped the bundle and grabbed him. "You know how much Tancy loves Jemmy." His collar muffled her words. He giggled and squirmed away from her embrace.

144

They walked on. The houses they passed were smaller now, and spaced farther apart.

"Will she buy me candy?"

"If she has the money to buy it with, she will. But even if mamas don't have money, they give their chaps everything they can, because they love them so much."

The high-minded talk made Jemmy restive. "Are we almost there?"

Tancy didn't know the answer to that one. Before, their walks had never taken them beyond the shops of what she innocently believed was a large city. Now already the town had petered out; the street they followed ended at a hillock of pines and jack oak crowding down to an unpainted cottage with a cistern at the door and chickens in the yard.

"We must be on the wrong street," she said.

"Can we go up there?" Jemmy pointed out a pathway that penetrated the woods.

"If you want to," said Tancy, and let him plunge ahead. Let him learn. If they did not find Shantytown today (or ever), if Shantytown simply could not be located, if it did not even exist, well . . .

The woods, menacing from the outside, dusty-light on the inside, crowded the town side of a hill that the path mounted. On the other side, large timber had been cut away recently, leaving a slope of stumps and scrub. The morning sun beat harshly on this ravaged landscape, but Tancy and Jemmy saw only the village that lay below them, a sprawl of ramshackle huts snaking along the sides of a ravine.

They had arrived at Shantytown.

15

A T FIRST THE PLACE seemed deserted; they heard no voices, saw no movement. Then, as they approached, they saw why. Their path entered Shantytown at its backside, through a break in the ragged row. They entered the alleyway and came out on a dirt street that ran along the topmost rank of shacks.

For a few merchants on this street, the work day had already begun. An elderly man straddled a crude cobbler's bench in front of his house and tapped away at his last. Close by, a woman hung strands of yellow-dyed wool in her open doorway. But it was still early in the day, and most of the other entrances were closed. Farther along the street a plump young woman untied a door curtain and let a toddler out to play. A slender, stern man wearing thick glasses appeared beside the plump woman and said something about the toddler that made her laugh.

What must it be like to live in a place like this? Tancy wondered. The red clay streets undoubtedly melted into muck whenever it rained; now, in drought time, they were stony underfoot. Across from where they stood she looked at a second row of huts strung together, facing a second dirt street lower down, and beyond, the stair-stepped roofs of still more dwellings. Narrow lanes here and there connected one terrace with another, and into one of these alleyways the toddler escaped in a precipitous trot. The plump young woman leaped after the youngster.

"Looky her," said Jemmy.

Tancy said, "Mm hm." Her eyes were on the stern man in glasses. She had never before seen a black man wear spectacles. At Gaither's, failing eyesight merely signaled a change of jobs, never the purchase of glasses. Aunt Lessie, who for forty years knitted all the stockings on the place, had been put to minding chaps and the ash hopper when her eyes gave out.

Jemmy twitched her skirt. "Her?" he questioned, in his little-boy treble.

The plump woman emerged from the alleyway with the baby tucked under her arm. "Get me a tether for this wild chap!" she shouted at the man in glasses, and smacked the child's bottom playfully. Mother and child made a jolly pair of chubbies. The woman's face dimpled at the early morning visitors.

Jemmy tugged at Tancy's skirt. "Is her my mammy?"

"No!" said Tancy forcefully, but her heart turned over in a sickish thud. Not so soon, not now. Mary wasn't a fat girl, part of her argued; but a more rational side registered the nubbin of chin in that round face, the dimples, the hair drawn to an intricate biscuit at the top of that head. "Mary," she faltered.

The woman continued to smile, examining Tancy's face in cordial puzzlement. "Do I know you, honey?"

Tancy looked down at the boy burrowing in her skirt. "Jemmy," she managed to say. "From Gaither's."

"Oh, my Lord," said Mary. She plopped the baby on the ground and seized Jemmy in her arms — or would have seized him, if Jemmy had not resisted.

"Jemmy?" said Mary, with tears starting from her eyes. She pried the little boy loose from Tancy's leg, and clutching him fiercely, she began screaming. "Lord, Lordy, Lord! Thank you, Jesus! Oh, my Lord, I prayed, I prayed so long!"

"Tancy!" Jemmy wailed.

Doors opened and curtains lifted and curious heads poked out to investigate the commotion. "My baby come home! Oh, my sweet little baby come home!" The whole town appeared to erupt, and almost instantly Tancy lost sight of Jemmy in the exclaiming mob that swirled around Mary. Yet above Mary's shrieks and the congratulatory cries of the others, she heard her darling's plea.

"Tancy!"

She started to work her way to him. "Let him go!" she screamed at Mary. Couldn't Mary see that he was scared, that he needed time? "Let him go, please!" But she couldn't get through to Mary, and the rejoicing went on; and presently she stood apart and wrestled with the cruel knowledge that Jemmy was her darling no longer. It was she, not Mary, who would have to let him go.

The excitement at last died down. The townspeople yielded enough for her to push into the throng. Before she could reach Jemmy, however, he caught sight of her, and waved, and satisfied that he had not lost her after all, began to relish his new role.

The toddler had been snatched up by the spectacled man when the crowd converged on Mary; and now the man, in response to something Mary told him, reached out and tousled Jemmy's head. Impartially, he cuddled and kissed the baby in his arms. A nice daddy, Tancy noted; showed more sense than Mary.

But he was not the baby's daddy, Mary said, when they got around to explanations. He was her brother, Henry, from Perquimans County. He came to Shantytown last year hunting Mary and stayed on to help her, she being alone with Bo, the baby. Mary reclaimed Bo from Henry and squeezed both children to her, gasping, "My babies! The Lord has blessed me, I got both my sweet babies!"

Henry twinkled behind those forbidding glasses. His lean jaw creased, and there for a moment he reminded Tancy of Mary in her younger years, carefree Mary, before Jemmy, before the trader. "Sis told my name, but I still don't know yours," he said.

"I'm Tancy," she said sedately, "from Gaither's."

Mary squealed. "Not Tancy! From the big house? No wonder I never recognized you, honey. Little Tancy! All growed up."

"Yes," said Tancy, "and you —"

"— run to fat," Mary finished for her, with a slap to her ample thigh. "Come in this house, honey, and let's us all get acquainted."

The back wall of Mary's house had been dug back into the fastness of the hill. Partitions of woven cane divided her dwelling from the ones on either side, and brush piled overhead roofed them all. The covering wouldn't stop any kind of a rain, Mary admitted, but precious little rain had fallen this year to test it.

She had built the place with her own hands, she boasted, and she pointed out its furnishings with pride: the water bucket, her collection of metal plates and spoons, an iron spider, the quilt she had pieced back at Marsters', south of Salisbury — all she had felt entitled to when she left Marsters'. There were valuables she had left behind, and she named these.

"They was a butter churn in my cabin (I done all the churning, see), but I knowed it rightfully belonged to Missus, so I left that. And a stewpot with a lid." She regretted most a beautiful picture of a lady with a bow-and-arrow in a painted frame, bestowed upon Mary the very day the man came around from the bureau and read them all the freedom paper.

Tancy murmured her admiration of Mary's belongings, both present and past, while silently she ached to think of Jemmy reduced to living in this hovel. For life! This was to be his life!

Henry said angrily, "You wouldn't have been given the picture if it wasn't for the freedom paper."

"Now, Henry." Mary gave a tolerant laugh. "You never knowed my old marse and miss. They wasn't like what you say. They give us all them things for love of us — we was like a family. I miss them yet," she confessed.

149

He rose from his seat on the floor and stamped about the tiny room. "You're a fool!" he exclaimed. "They didn't give you those things, they owed them to you, them and a lot more!" In the tiny hut, he seemed to fill the room. It was the glasses, Tancy thought, a bit awed. She wished she could somehow get Jemmy off Mary's lap. He sat there swaying hypnotically as Mary's fingers languidly stroked his back.

"The greatest thing in all the world has happened to our people!" cried Henry. "And all you can think of is your damned picture and how generous old marse was to give it to you."

Mary would not be intimidated by him. "Oh, Henry," she chided, "you just don't know. 'Twas easy for y'all, over in Perquimans." (Stroke, stroke. Jemmy swayed, with half-closed eyes.)

"It was not easy!" the man roared. "I had to sneak and grin and pretend like everybody else, before freedom. But not after, no ma'am, not after. Never again for me!" He jerked the door curtain aside and strode out of the hut.

Mary continued stroking Jemmy's back. "Easy for a fellow out on his own to talk. Whole nother thing for me, with a chap to feed and raise and nobody to help me do it. Course, Henry been giving me money along, since he come, but his money ain't gonna last, the way he spends it. Well, he ain't no better'n a chap hisself."

A chap! To Tancy, Henry had seemed the essence of maturity.

No indeed, Mary said. Henry was her *baby* brother, baby by a month – a half brother – and she didn't intend to let him forget it, regardless of how he strutted around in those boss specs and talked against her old marse.

"Exact same time he's excusing that old sinner what's wringing every penny she can out of us poor folks," Mary exclaimed. "It's a sin, what she does. I vow they call her right, Sin, having to do with her old master right here in Shantytown; if that ain't sinful! Henry, he won't hear aught spoke against her, but if I speak respectful of my old marse once — well, you heard him holler yourself."

Tancy had little interest in some old woman she didn't even know, sinful or otherwise. Her eyes rested on Jemmy, in Mary's lap. Mary taking him over so completely didn't suit Tancy; it didn't suit Bo either. He plucked at his mother and he plucked at Jemmy's shirt, and when Mary swatted him, he fell down and bawled for a while, and when he got tired of bawling, he got up and started picking at Jemmy again.

"He's hungry, I spect." Mary shifted Jemmy to one side. She fumbled a breast up out of her dress and allowed Bo to stand between her knees and nurse.

Tancy was appalled. That Bo was too old to be nursing still. Standing up! And Jemmy looking on!

For his part, Jemmy stared in amazement, and then flapped his hand in Bo's face. Bo rolled a malevolent eye.

Why was Mary allowing all this to happen? The situation ought to be managed delicately, and Jemmy introduced by degrees to this coarse life. Tancy said diplomatically, "I think I'll take Jemmy back to the bureau now, and bring him for short visits along, until he gets accustomed."

"Take him back to the bureau?" Mary first looked astonished, then she laughed comfortably. "Oh no, honey, we not gonna do that, no, no."

At that moment, Henry thrust his head in the door and said abruptly to Tancy, "You mentioned you're a teacher; you want to go look at my school?"

She scrambled to her feet. "I didn't realize you had a school. Yes! Let's go look at the school, Jemmy!"

"My don't want to go to school," Jemmy whined, staring at Bo.

"Stop talking babyish," Tancy snapped. She felt like smacking him.

"But him *is* a baby," Mary declared. She gathered Jemmy close. "Him's his mama's sugar baby."

"Leave them alone," Henry advised. "Give them a chance to get used to each other."

He led Tancy swiftly along the terrace and through a number of lanes threading the maze that was Shantytown. The place was lively now. Women bent over laundry at the bottom of the ravine, where despite the drought a shallow stream ran. Tancy picked her way across on stepping stones that rimmed a dammed-up pool where a steady traffic of young girls came to dip their buckets.

Higher up on one of the opposite terraces, a white man unexpectedly confronted Tancy. "Are you the wet nurse I hired yesterday?" he demanded. "The baby's been crying since dawn. If my wife can't depend on you —"

"Across the branch and all the way to the top on the other side," Henry directed him. "Ask for Mary." To Tancy he said caustically, "You black girls all look alike to him."

Tancy, like fat Mary? "Where is your school?" she asked curtly.

Up the hill, he told her, on the sunrise side of Shantytown, where the new houses were. Mary lived in the old part.

Old and new, the dwellings of Shantytown were constructed of waste materials. Some were of woven cane, like Mary's, but most were of poles and scrap lumber pieced together, or of odds and ends of rusting metal. No two were alike, yet all looked depressingly the same.

To Henry, the town was beautiful. Here lived people who wanted off the plantation, and were striking out at last on their own. Here you could hire any kind of work you wanted done, he bragged. Already you could buy all manner of goods in small shops.

The hill they were climbing leveled out and they came upon a neat log cabin, small, but snugly fitted, and standing apart in a yard of its own fenced with railings. A chimney of unmortared fieldstones rose outside the dwelling at one end, and on either side of the low front door two tiny glassed windows peered at passersby.

152

Not only the windows surveyed them. An oddly garbed old woman shot out the door as they approached and shook her fist at Tancy. "Pay me my money, you trifling piece!" she squalled. "Ain't nobody moves onto my property thout paying for it. Thout asking leave! What kind of raising you had, girl?"

Henry laughed. "You girls look alike to her too," he said to Tancy; and to the woman: "You're accusing the wrong girl, Sin. Tancy is only here for the day, visiting my sister."

The woman came close and said, "Don't you try to cheat me, girl. It don't pay. I find out every time." A tortoiseshell comb trembled in her meager, graying hair.

"You've got Tancy mixed up with somebody else, Sin," said Henry. "She brought my sister's little boy to her, from Gaither's, where Mary was sold away from. You mustn't accuse Tancy of cheating you."

The woman squinted mistrustfully. "Tancy?" She worked her lips, as if she were prepared to spit out something tainted. It was impossible to tell how old she was, the way she screwed up her face. That might even have been a pretty, pouty mouth, once.

"Gaither's?" the old woman pondered, fingering her shawl. It was rather an elegant shawl, fringed, made of shiny ecru cloth and decorated with sprigs of lilac flowers. She hugged it around a brown poplin dress trimmed with lace and jet buttons, protected from soil by a coarse striped coverall; and the coverall in turn was protected by a dingy white apron. She removed the comb from her hair and muttered over it. Then she gestured with it at Tancy and said querulously, "You move in with Mary, you still got to pay rent to me, not her, you understand?"

"Yes ma'am," said Tancy meekly. She didn't like this old woman, still she could not speak uncivilly to her. "I'm not moving in with Mary or anybody else. I just came to bring my, to bring — her — little boy."

The woman sniffed disagreeably and went back inside her cabin.

"She's not as bad as she sounds," Henry said, ready to argue.

"It's her land, after all. Our people still haven't got used to the idea that they've got to pay for freedom."

"Mm-n," said Tancy.

"Sin doesn't overcharge them. She's got to make her living, too."

"I'm sure."

"Her old master gave her the land after freedom, and he still comes to see her; that's the thing they resent. Seems to me it's only natural for him to take an interest in her welfare. They gossip about him coming around, but I say it's jealousy."

By now Tancy had got her fill of Sin. "I hope we get to your school soon," she said pointedly.

Henry ran ahead to a large, decently built wooden structure. He flung open its door and presented his school, a big roomful of students sitting on long benches and attending to a white woman who moved among them checking written work and assigning lessons. The woman wore a mobcap like Miss Michaels's. She acknowledged the visitors with a slight nod and went on with her teaching.

Tancy had to admire the school. Who wouldn't? A place that looked like a real schoolroom? The books were new, the slates unbroken. "It's really nice," she admitted to Henry.

He took off his glasses and blinked gratefully. "You like it? Did you notice the slates? Pencils for everybody, look!" He snatched a slate pencil from a tiny girl and brandished it. "They're all learning to write. Write!" he commanded the girl, returning her pencil. "Show how you can write."

He rushed about the room to point out its modern features, the window with glass panes at one end, the desks, the long benches that could be used as church pews, the cupboard with extra books inside; and all the while, in a flood of words, he related the circumstances of its construction. He it was who had conceived the idea of a school for the people of Shantytown, he who planned it, hired the builders, bought the books, located the teacher.

154

It was Henry too who paid for everything — and here he digressed to explain where the money came from. His master, back in Perquimans County, was a lawyer who saw to Henry's education and put him to clerking in his office. He knew more about the law than his master did, Henry claimed. The master paid his clerk a salary long before the Federals came around to make him do it, begged Henry with tears in his eyes not to leave him, after freedom, but gave him a hundred dollars and said he'd always find a home with Marse, whenever he felt like coming back.

Sh-h, Tancy wanted to tell him; you're disrupting the class. Mary had been right. There was something immature about this young man, striding among the wide-eyed students, caught up in his passion. His eyes glittered. His words were like pellets, bouncing off the walls. She could not decide whether she thought him inspiring or merely irritating. There was no question as to what the teacher felt.

"Be kind enough to continue your discussion outside, sir," she said, taking Henry firmly by the elbow.

Tancy gladly escaped through the door, but Henry followed her without haste. "You're doing a fine job, ma'am," he told the teacher, beaming. "Is there anything at all you want, anything the pupils need?"

"Well, I hope the stove is going to get here pretty soon," the teacher said forcefully. "Some of these mornings are quite cool, and they won't get any warmer, with November on the way."

"The stove's ordered, it's coming, don't you worry about it," Henry assured her.

After she had closed the door on them, he told Tancy, "She won't last out another fortnight. Fourth teacher we've had since the school opened." He seemed unconcerned over the impending loss, although he conceded that she was a fine teacher. They didn't last, these Yankee ladies. They came out of their schools and churches in the North full of energy and ideas, all ready to enlighten the South; but the first enlightenment was their own:

no white family would take them in. "This one's boarding at Sin's, and she's held out better than the others."

But that arrangement would end soon, Henry predicted. The teacher complained about the sanitary arrangements and criticized Sin's cooking. She accused her of snooping through her things, and she alienated the old lady by curtaining off her end of the cabin from Sin's.

As Henry talked, they retraced their steps along the path by which they had come. They encountered Sin before they reached her cabin. She waited, a forbidding figure in the pathway, and she seemed still determined upon a quarrel. She placed her hands on her hips, and when Tancy drew near enough to meet her eye, she said accusingly, "Claim you from Gaither's?"

"I used to be, yes ma'am," said Tancy. "I've been staying at the bureau in town lately."

"Say they call you Tancy?"

"That's my name, yes ma'am."

"Who's your pappy, girl?"

Tancy stiffened. "My father's dead."

"Dead don't take away his name, do it?" said the woman irritably. Since their first meeting, she had tied colored ribbons around her head. An enameled brooch now fastened her shawl, and a beaded reticule swung from a cord passed around her waist. She touched her hair from time to time as she spoke. Like a woman worried about her appearance, Tancy reflected. Like a woman fixed up to impress somebody.

Sin said, "Child, don't you know your own pappy's name?"

None of your business, Tancy longed to retort. Instead, some authority in the old woman compelled her to answer, "Master was my father – Mas Gaither."

The woman released a sharp breath. "Well, take a good look at me, girl. I'm your mammy."

156

16

TWO CHILDREN DAWDLING on the path to eavesdrop tittered. Sin yelled a threat to send them scampering and hurried Tancy and Henry back to her cabin.

"Go on, go in." She prodded them through the door. Inside she thrust a wooden lock pin through the latch, and drew green taffeta curtains over the windows. With a turkey wing, she brushed ashes from the coals in her fireplace and teased out a flame with twigs from her kindling basket. She peered into the swing kettle hanging to one side, added a dipperful of water, and guided it over the fire. "I got some coffee," she announced. "Y'all want coffee?"

"Yes, please," said Tancy. Her head swam. She tried to think how to inform the old woman that she was wrong. Even her name was wrong. *Sin!* Tancy's mother was Lulu, and she could prove it by the ledger at Gaither's Mill. This farcical reunion was some kind of mistake, her mind said.

"... mistake?" Henry was asking the woman.

"No mistake," said Sin offhandedly. She might have been commenting on the weather. She clasped a dome of loaf sugar to her chest and bending over a huge knife, sliced a measure of sugar into each of three cups on the table. Two of the cups were china; the third was metal and lacked a handle. "No mistake. Look at her eyes, no whites to them, just like mine. Soul eyes, folks used to say. I'd knowed her anywheres. Says herself she's called Tancy, no mistake about that."

"But I know a couple of girls named Tancy in Perquimans County." The world was full of Tancys, Henry implied.

Sin ignored him. "She were Nancy first. I given her the name, but Miss Puddin wun't let her carry it. 'Twas the same as Master's first wife, she were a Nancy too, and that wun't've did. That's how come her to be Tancy, not to make no trouble twixt him and Miss Puddin. He were boss at Gaither's, but everbody knowed Miss Puddin, she were bossier." Sin whinnied.

Tancy managed at last to speak. "What did they call *you*, back then?"

Sin shrugged. "*He* callt me Lulu. My whole name be Lucinda."

Sin, Lucinda. Oh, Mother, Tancy grieved, already yearning for the lost mother of her dreams. How could she give up the Lulu she had fashioned in her mind — soft, sweet Lulu, beloved of Mas Gaither?

Sin pointed a spoon at the swing kettle. "Coffee's ready. Set and drink it." She poured a muddy beverage from the kettle into the three cups and they seated themselves at a narrow plank table. Henry sat on one of its benches, Tancy and Sin sat side by side on the other. Sin shuffled the cups to suit some honorary order in her mind. Henry got the metal cup. Sin took the cracked cup for herself. Tancy was awarded the fancy cup with the baroque handle.

It was dreadful coffee; Tancy recognized the parched-corn brew that slaves called coffee. This potful, left over from breakfast, watered down and served tepid, celebrated what should have been a poignant moment. Tancy sat in aching silence, hating the moment, hating the coffee, hating Sin. At least the woman had not offered to kiss her.

Out of the long silence, Sin croaked, "The missus, she callt me *Her*."

Henry lifted his cup with a smile and toasted the occasion. He complimented them both. He spoke of their future together. He sounded like somebody at a wedding! At last he drained his cup with an elaborate show of savoring the coffee and announced his intention of leaving mother and daughter by themselves, so they could "get caught up."

Tancy leaped to her feet. "I'd better go with you. I need to see about Jemmy."

"Jemmy's got his own mama to look after him," Henry reminded her. "You and your mama just sit here and relax and enjoy yourselves."

But she didn't intend for this domineering young man to take charge of her life. "I only asked for enough time off to bring Jemmy here," she said politely. "They're expecting me back at the bureau. I really must go."

"That you'll not," Sin said strongly. (Two of them!) "I vow you already done more for that birro place than they done for you or anybody else."

Henry said, "Sin's right. What has the bureau really done to help? Promised our people forty acres and a mule, and nobody's seen either yet."

"I don't want any forty acres," said Tancy, beginning to tremble. She had to get away from this pair. "All I want is my job."

"Don't worry about your job," said Henry. "This is a great day! Enjoy it!" He had to go into the town, anyway, to check up on the school stove, he said. It would be no trouble at all for him to stop in at the bureau and tell them Tancy wanted a few more days off. He knew they wouldn't begrudge her the time, hearing she'd found her long-lost mother. They'd be happy for her.

Happier than me, Tancy thought dismally

Henry unlocked Sin's door and poked his head outside. "Looks like good news travels fast."

A crowd of Shantytown's residents stood outside the fence railings. Tancy felt beaten. How would it look for her to walk away from a long-lost mother through that mob?

Sin, like a multicolored whirlwind, spun into the yard. "Y'all out here to catch a mess of flies?" she shrilled.

Indeed, standing there goggle-eyed and greedy, the crowd might have been frogs lined at a pond's edge, awaiting a tidbit. One bold woman called out, "Chirren say your girl come."

"What if she did? Get out of my yard! Leave the child settle before y'all start nibbling at her the way you do me."

"Now, Sin," said Henry.

The watchers began to disperse, mumbling among themselves and moving deliberately so as not to appear driven off.

"Go on!" Sin snatched the ribbons from her head and flapped them. "Get out of here!" She looked like a disreputable old parrot, flapping and screeching.

My *mother?* Tancy despaired.

Sin took charge. She ordered Tancy into the house and secured the latch. Tancy was not to peek out from behind the curtains, she said, or to have any truck with that shiftless bunch outside. Half of them owed her money; why weren't they working, so they could pay their honest debts, instead of meddling around her house?

The party was obviously over. Sin unpinned her brooch and removed the beaded reticule, which she placed beside her hair ribbons on the bed.

"Watch where I put these," she told Tancy. "It'll all be yours when I'm gone." She kept her treasures in an old stocking under the mattress, "where nobody would think to look," as she explained it.

At noontime, Sin went out to get water, leaving Tancy to put their dinner on the table. A narrow pine dresser with a hinged cupboard and a metal-covered shelf held plates and spoons and the cabin's store of foodstuffs. Tancy set the table with two plates. She divided a wedge of cornbread into two portions. She divided the cold cooked bacon. She laid spoons beside the two plates, and then she stood looking into the fireplace until Sin came back with the water.

Sin poured up what was left of the day's coffee. "Set and eat," she said. Mother and daughter faced each other across the plank table for their first meal together.

"Eat up," Sin pressed her. "That bacon come from my master's smokehouse. You won't never eat no better."

Tancy crumbled the cornbread and mashed the bacon with her spoon. The morsel she swallowed seemed to stick and swell in her gullet. "I'm not very hungry," she said.

Sin nodded. "Saving your figger. I did too, when I was your age. You got my figger."

Tancy thought, No, I don't. I don't have your eyes and I don't have your figure. I don't look anything like you.

"Oh, I watched out for my figger, them days," Sin continued. "'I ain't hungry,' I'd say. Mammy'd say to me, 'Them that don't eat dinner don't get they supper.'"

"Your mother — " Tancy's curiosity won out. "My grand-mother?"

"Your granny, yes. Never lived to see but one of her grand-children. Go-Charlie, she saw him; he were my first."

"Go-Charlie! I remember hearing about Go-Charlie from Uncle Swamp."

"That old cuss."

"Tell me what Grandmother was like."

Sin stopped the spoon halfway to her mouth — her mother? Dead for so many years, it was hard to remember. "Turble," she said in amazement. "Her and me never set saddle together some-hows. She was a fieldhand, see, and I was shamed of how she look, all knobhanded and bunchwaist. She were a good woman,

161

I know that now; but being the way it goes, a gal with her mammy, I'd ruther she keep her good to herself."

"You told your mother that?" Tancy was shocked.

"No, child!" Sin, in turn, was shocked. "I knowed better than to sass her. It was 'Yes, Mammy,' and 'No, Mammy,' whatever she say. Chirren was *respectful* of they folks them days. And then," Sin added with a glint, "when she look away, I go do what I want."

Dishonest, Tancy noted, feeling virtuous. "Tell me about Alexander and Go-Charlie," she said. "Tell me about my brothers."

"Half brothers," Sin corrected. "They was outside chirren, hatched a heap before you was." Alexander and Go-Charlie had met and married sisters in South Carolina, she said; two uppity women who turned their husbands against their own mother. "I hope your ears never hear such as they call me," the old woman said bitterly. "Call you them names too."

"Me?" Tancy's mouth fell open. "They don't even know me. Why would they call me names?"

"Cause you got Marse Gaither's blood, child."

"But I couldn't help that!"

"Me neither."

For a silent space the two sat, pondering the injustice that united them.

"They was two baby girls too, half sisters of you. One of em born dead, one died fore she's walking." Sin sighed. "You're all the chick and child I got left in this world now."

Tancy had to know. "Who was the daddy of the little girls?"

"My master — Marse Rankin. My good marse," said Sin proudly. "He give me my house and my land when freedom come; he been good to me, Marse Rankin has."

Tancy felt a chill. "That wouldn't be Herbert Rankin, would it? That lives next to the Shuford plantation?"

"That's him. Hub Rankin." Sin pointed out the furnishings Master Rankin had given her — the dresser and dishes, the carpet, the green taffeta curtains, and her prize, the iron bedstead that stood against the wall. He had always been good to her and never denied her, even while Mistress was living, Sin boasted. So she did not deny him, now that freedom was upon her. It mattered not that her tenants gossiped about her and complained about the rents she charged. It was her land, and if they thought the rents were too high, they could look for another place to live. "If it be their land, they do the same," Sin said. "They jealous, is all."

The food lay uneaten on their plates as Sin related what her life had been since leaving Gaither's Mill — the two of them got caught up, as Henry had told them to.

When school let out in the afternoon, the teacher beat on the barred door and Sin let her in. The woman, without speaking, retired behind her curtained end of the cabin. Sin winked at Tancy and tilted her nose with a forefinger to pantomime what she thought of the teacher. "High-toned."

Later on Henry stopped by to report on his trip into Knoxford. "I left word at the bureau you'd be back in a week or two," he said airily. "They don't care. I told you they wouldn't."

Tancy said, "You spoke to Miss Michaels?"

"No, it was some lieutanant that didn't know B from bull's foot. I had to ask three people before I could find your room and pack up your clothes." He handed her a bundle. "I thought you'd be needing these."

Tancy said crushingly, "They put that chain across the stairs, and the sign, to keep people out of the dormitory."

"It never kept you out, did it?"

"Of course not. I lived there! At night I just unhooked the chain and went up."

He said tolerantly, "That's what I did. It wasn't hard to figure out."

She kept her temper. In a tight voice she said, "I'm going to go and see about Jemmy."

"Not now," said Sin. "You got to help me set supper."

"Anyway, Jemmy's not there," said Henry. "Mary took him into town with her."

"Then I'll wait for him to get back," Tancy flared.

For a wonder, they did not contradict her, and she let herself out of the cabin and sped along the terrace in the direction she supposed Mary's house to be. Twice she passed through the same alleyway, hunting for the return route. A woman dashed out of a patchwork hovel and offered to buy the shirtwaist off her back. (Miss Michaels's shirtwaist!) People crowded the narrow terraces.

She saw shops that had not been open this morning, tiny grocery stores with turnips and beets and gourd measures of shelled corn for sale or barter. She saw a blacksmith hammering straight a collection of bent nails, a medicine man with his roots and herbs displayed in piles on a plank counter.

She found a new alleyway and asked a civil-looking woman the way to Mary's house, and managed to arrive there just as the little family returned from the town. Bo hung limp asleep under Mary's arm. They had all gone in together to her wet-nurse job; the family lived close by, she said, so it made it easy for her, and she could stay at home in between feedings and tend to her own children. She made it sound as though Jemmy had been living with her forever. When Mary went inside to put Bo down, Tancy couldn't wait to get her hands on Jemmy.

"Tancy's Jemmy," she whispered, showering kisses across his face and hugging him urgently before Mary came back to reclaim him.

"Um-m," Jemmy agreed placidly, licking sticky, dirty hands.

"Mary bought you candy, I see," she said.

"She bought me marbles too," He showed her the beauties. One aggie, two milkies, and a glassy. "She's going to buy me more tomorrow."

"She's going to buy *you*," said Tancy bitterly.

Mary came out of her hut smiling. "Didn't take this little boy no time at all to cotton up to his mama," she declared.

"I'm sure," said Tancy.

"Come on in and eat supper with us; it's about that time."

"Thank you. I'm supposed to eat at Sin's tonight."

"At Sin's! Don't tell me that stingy old crook invited you to eat with her!"

"That stingy old crook," said Tancy, "happens to be my mother." She had the satisfaction of seeing Mary's shocked face before she flounced away.

But she wished she might choke, hurrying back across the ravine. *Mother,* she had called Sin, not for love, but for spite.

She was ordered to sleep in the iron bedstead with Sin that night, although she protested most sincerely that she preferred to sleep on the floor.

"Ain't no daughter of mine sleeping on no floor, and her mammy in the bedstead," Sin said.

"Why not?" the teacher called out furiously. It was the first time she had spoken all evening long. "You never slept in the bedstead before."

"I never had my daughter here before," Sin replied smugly.

Tancy undid the parcel of clothing that Henry had brought. There were her chemise, her nightgown, the shawl Miss Michaels had given her, and her clean underdrawers. Who had made up that bundle? "I thought you'd be needing these," she remembered Henry saying.

She tried not to think about it. It was no use. Lying miserably on her side of the bed, unable to sleep, she alternately brooded about Jemmy and squirmed at the image of Henry, folding and smoothing her underdrawers. It was almost as though he touched her, with those shapely law-clerk hands of his, touched her in the most intimate way. Nasty! She hated him!

The five nights she spent with Sin exhausted her; the days were torment. Mary's job and Sin's routine conspired, it seemed, to keep Jemmy from her, and their few unsatisfactory meetings left her more and more depressed. Her little boy, growing away from her! It hurt her that he adopted this new life so easily.

On Saturday Sin took her along with her to collect her weekly rents. "My daughter," she introduced Tancy everywhere. "This here's my girl, what I ain't seen since she's a baby. That's ten cents you owe me." Tancy trailed behind her, groggy from lack of sleep and preoccupied with her thoughts of Jemmy.

When they returned from their rounds, they found a sheet of letter paper on the plank table, covered with handwriting that looked like Miss Michaels's. For a heady instant, Tancy dreamed it was a letter from Miss Michaels, that her dear friend had written to claim her, to take her away from here. But in the same instant she realized that it must be a message from the teacher. And so it was. Sin grabbed the coins that weighted the paper.

"Say what it say! Tell what it say!" she clamored. A letter of her own! And a daughter of her own to read the letter — a daughter who could read anything, everything!

Madam:

Please be advised that I shall no longer require space in your house, as I have left off teaching in the school today's date. Mr. Henry understands and concurs with my decision, and I am sure you too will appreciate that my situation here has not been ideal. Board in full herewith for month of October (50 cents).

Sin rushed to inspect the curtained area the teacher had vacated. She pulled the stocking from its hiding place under the mattress and checked its contents. "Ain't nothing been stole that I can see."

"Why would you suspect her of stealing?" said Tancy. "She paid you what she owed you."

Sin sniffed. "You can't trust them teacher-women."

166

Tancy was disgusted. "You say that just because you didn't like her."

Sin nodded her agreement. "Didn't like her from the time I seen her. Good gone to her, I say. I don't need her board money."

Tancy gritted her teeth. It was true Sin didn't need the teacher any longer — she had a daughter to bully now. And as if Sin weren't enough to contend with, the officious Henry turned up to do his share when they went to Mary's house that afternoon.

Jemmy, today the owner of six new marbles and a penny poke of candy, had become an important fellow in Shantytown. A crowd of small boys surrounded him, and he refused to come when Tancy called.

Henry said, "Let him alone. He's busy getting acquainted."

"He's busy getting spoiled," Tancy retorted, out of her hurt.

Mary gazed fondly on her little boy, at the center of his world. "That's what chirren are for, to spoil."

"He shouldn't eat all that candy," Tancy objected.

"A penny's worth won't hurt him. Besides, he said you bought him candy all the time." Bought him enough to make him sick, her tone accused.

Tancy said, "Children ought to *share*, is what I meant. That's my experience as a schoolteacher."

Henry took her elbow. "Suppose you and I have a little talk about that, Tancy, and about Jemmy."

"No, thanks!" She yanked away and scowled at him. She wasn't going to take any more lecturing from Henry.

"Guess what, the teacher's quit!" Sin put in, bursting to tell the news. "She snuck out whilst I was out of the house."

Tancy turned on her. "She didn't sneak! She left a note!"

"She didn't even have the nerve to tell me to my face," said Sin.

Henry said diplomatically that he had been expecting the woman to leave for some time. Although her departure might seem hasty to Sin, the teacher had given him notice of her intention yesterday,

167

candidly and openly; and the two of them had parted without rancor.

"I was about to propose that Tancy replace her," Henry continued. "Her presence in the classroom would mean so much to Jemmy, at this critical time. But it seems she doesn't care to discuss the matter."

"Teach the school yourself," Tancy snapped. "You're so good at everything." She stalked off, filled with rage and pain, and blaming him for the misunderstanding.

Sin caught up with her halfway home. "You done right," she commended her. "You don't want to stick in no schoolhouse. Get out in the town, start you a little trade; I'll stake you. Trade is where the money's at."

"I don't care about the money."

"Course you do. Everybody does. Only thing you can depend on in this world."

For you, maybe; not for me, Tancy would have countered at another time. But she couldn't dispute anymore, she felt so low.

Furthermore, lying in the bed that night, she decided that Sin was probably right. All the people Tancy loved had either died or disappointed her in one way or another, so why not put your faith in money, that constant friend?

"You got enough covers up there?" Sin shouted from her pallet on the floor. She must be growing deaf, Tancy realized with a twinge of remorse.

"Fine," she shouted back. Sin's concern for her comfort touched and warmed her. She felt a bit drowsy, too, after all the wakeful, miserable nights. Having the bed to herself tonight helped. The mother had overridden Tancy's objections to this new arrangement — nothing more to prove, now that her enemy, the teacher, had gone.

What a funny creature Sin was, Tancy mused, half asleep, almost at peace. The mother's determination to pamper her child had diluted all that spite and greed. She was like Mary that way. Like Miss Puddin.

Poor Miss Puddin (Tancy's thoughts eddied, floated into dreaming). Who was there for Miss Puddin to pamper, now that Billy was gone?

17

S HE AWOKE THE NEXT morning feeling rested and in rising
spirits. It had rained during the night, and the break in the
long drought made her hope for a break in her luck. It was
Sunday. They must go to church, Sin said, and thank the Lord
for his blessings.

"What blessings?" Tancy gibed.

"Freedom!" said Sin. "The church!" and Tancy felt properly
rebuked.

Sin heated a smoothing iron in the fireplace, and Tancy pressed
both their dresses in observance of the occasion. She wasted her
labor. Sodden grass and weeds beside the path whipped their
skirts as they picked their way to the schoolhouse, where church
services were held. Scarcely a roof in Shantytown had withstood
the rain. A damp but cheerful congregation jammed the room to
hear the preacher "read" Scripture out of his hands.

"The good book says, 'In Jesus there's no man nor woman,
good nor bad, old nor young,'" he intoned. "We're all one and
the same to the Master."

"Amen," said Sin.

There was a Bible on the table behind the preacher, and he touched it humbly to indicate that the sacred words had been transferred from it to his palms. This gentle illiterate reminded Tancy of the one who used to come around, summers, to Gaither's Mill. In lay-by time that preacher held evening revival meetings in the locust grove down by the barn; and although he was not allowed even to possess a Bible, someone always lighted a torch of fat pine as the night came on, so that the preacher could see to "read" out of his hands.

Often the Gaithers would sit on the back porch listening. Tancy and Julia listened too, sitting on the floor beside the two rocking chairs. The preacher's words were barely audible to those on the porch; Tancy usually just listened to the rhythms of his voice.

Here in the schoolhouse, she heard those resonances again, and she drifted into reverie. . . . There would be cicadas tuning up, she remembered, and the harsh clacking of guineas going to roost. Across the evening sky she would see the leap and plunge of swallows feeding on night insects, as the fingers of pines reached for the lowering sun.

An almost forgotten sweetness welled within her. Beautiful Gaither's Mill. She thought of Stud, begging her to go back there with him. "A pretty place," she heard him saying again, in his honest way. She wished she had been kinder to Stud.

"The Lord heard my prayers, yes, He did." Mary stood in the aisle to testify.

"Yes, He did," the congregation insisted.

"Yes, He did," affirmed the preacher.

"I prayed to God!" Mary shrieked. Her eyes closed in ecstasy. "And he brought my Jemmy back to me!"

Tancy emerged from her trance. *I* brought him back to her, she thought coldly. Then hands unexpectedly grabbed and propelled her into the aisle beside Mary.

"Sent my baby boy back to me," Mary screeched in her ear,

"in the blessed arms of this precious sister!" She pressed a fierce wet smack on Tancy's cheek.

"Praise the Lord. Praise Him."

"Thank you, Sir!"

Sin jumped to her feet and lifted Tancy's hand high with her own. "Thank you, Lord, for my baby girl!" Her stern countenance dared the congregation. "This here's my girl, folks, that I was sold off from, whiles she were still a sucking baby. Whose work is it, folks, that she been returned to her mammy, and bring Mary's baby back to her at the same time?"

"Lord Jesus' work," the preacher boomed.

"Lord Jesus' work!" cried Mary.

"Thank you, Lord, thank you, Lord Jesus," the congregation chanted.

Tancy swallowed, moved by the rapture of the crowd. The preacher came into the aisle to shake her hand. Women reached out to touch her. From across the room, Henry's eyes asked hers a question. She looked away with an ache in her throat.

After church, Henry came to stand by her side, as if by tacit understanding that they might begin anew. The congregation swirled about her. People thronged to invite her and Sin to enter into their fellowship. It was as though all the old grudges had dissolved in the emotion of the moment.

"Let me just show you what I'm planning for the school," Henry said, as the crowd dwindled. "You didn't get much of a look before."

"I'll go on ahead and set dinner," Sin told Tancy; and she muttered in her ear, "Don't let Henry talk you into nothing."

The schoolhouse-church was built on Sin's property, Henry stressed. Although the old lady was not especially religious, she had appreciated the people's need for a church of their own, after the long years of worship in white churches. "She hasn't charged us any rent for it so far, but she'll probably get around to it." His eyes twinkled.

He showed her where the new stove was to go, and where an opening would be cut to the annex. Oh, he had big plans for Shantytown's school. It would become an institute someday, with agricultural and trades departments, and a normal school to train all the teachers they were going to need. He had already the promise of a Knoxford merchant's library, and he planned a trip to Raleigh before Christmas to learn what he could about accreditation and raising funds for the new institute.

"Our people will pay what they can; it'll be all ours," said Henry. "Now, please, won't you consider teaching here? We really need our own people to make this work, our own faculty."

Our people. Our faculty. He talked like a preacher reading out of his hands, carried away with his own zeal. She had to respect his enthusiasm; but she said noncommitally, "I'd better go before Sin comes to fetch me."

The peas that had simmered all night had already been dished up, and Sin was raking ashcake from the fireplace when they arrived at her cabin. She invited Henry to eat with them and dealt charred cabbage-leaf packets onto each plate. "Set and eat whiles it's hot," she said nervously. She had tied the colored ribbons around her head since church, Tancy noted, and she was wearing her brooch.

"All dressed up," Henry remarked.

Sin ignored him. "You ain't eating your ashcake, Tancy. You don't like ashcake?"

"I do like it. I am eating it." Tancy smeared her portion around on the tin plate. It was hot, as Sin said, but it was also half baked; the old woman could surely see the gluey mess that oozed from the packet and mingled with the peas.

"Eat that, it's just a little runny," Sin coaxed. "Ashcake ain't no good if you cook the life out of it. Y'all hurry up and eat."

Henry said, "What's the rush, Sin? You expecting a gentleman friend?"

"Huh!" she snorted, shoveling in peas. In fact, she had not

cleaned her plate before the door rattled under a ponderous knock.

"Oh, my land, it's him already!" Sin leaped up and flew about the cabin, gathering up Tancy's belongings. "Here." She wadded the clothes together and piled them into the girl's hands. "You better sleep over to Mary's tonight." She smoothed her apron, and fingering her ribbons, she opened the door to the white man who stood outside.

He was a thin, elderly fellow of medium height, bent in the shoulders, like a man suppressing a cough. He wore shapeless black trousers and a soiled white shirt with a string passed around the collar in lieu of a tie. Orange stains mottled his gray chin whiskers, and he tongued a brown quid of tobacco aside as he opened his mouth to speak.

"Got company, hay ye?" he asked.

Sin's fingers dug between Tancy's shoulder blades. She said, "These folks just leaving. Go on, y'all." She urged them outside and shut herself in with the farmer. Almost at once the door opened again and Sin flung out one last garment that she had overlooked: Tancy's spare underdrawers. She snatched them up, mortified.

Henry knew about every stitch she ever wore, she thought. It was Henry who had smoothed and folded these very drawers, Henry who had fetched them to her with a smile: "I thought you'd be needing these." Ah, he knew everything, sly Henry.

Her old master counted high with Sin, Henry was saying. He strode close behind Tancy on the path. Well, Hub Rankin wasn't a bad fellow. He'd lost his boys, one at Shiloh and the other at Vicksburg, and his wife died of grief, it was said, for her children were her life; there was a daughter that nobody mentioned anymore, who had married a Yankee and moved up north. "You know the old man's lonely. Sin's all the family he's got left."

"Family."

"Hub means a lot to her too."

"Yes, she's got herself a nice bedstead," Tancy said nastily.

"Be fair," Henry reprimanded. "Sin's had a hard life. She went to South Carolina three times after freedom, hunting her boys. Twice on foot. And after she found them, they wouldn't have anything to do with her. I'm sure that's why she didn't look you up — she couldn't bear any more pain."

Pain? Tough old Sin. Tancy wanted to laugh. She had to laugh. But it came out more like a sob. She ran ahead with her armful of clothing jammed against her mouth.

"Where are you going? This isn't the way to Mary's."

"I'm not going to Mary's. I'm going back to the bureau."

He caught up with her on the slope above Shantytown. "Are you sure you want to go back?"

"Very sure."

"You don't have to live at Sin's, if that's what's bothering you," he said. "We'll find you another place, fix you up a place at the school, if you'd like to teach — "

Mary had been right. Henry was exactly like a child, scheming to get his way. His eyes saucered like a child's, behind those thick lenses.

She said loftily, "I already have a place. I teach at the bureau."

"But that's *their* place, not ours. In Shantytown, you'd be working for our people."

Our people again. "I work for our people at the bureau, if you want to know."

He said gravely, "Tancy, listen to me. The bureau is so sure our people are going to cheat them that they don't use what money they've got to help. They spend it keeping records instead. How many people have they offered more than a meal or a dose of medicine or a ticket to Arkansas? Do you call that helping?"

"Yes, I do," she flared, "I certainly do!"

"Oh, you're so stubborn," he said. "You're just like your mother."

It was too much. She wasn't like Sin, didn't talk, think, or look like her. She screamed at him, "You leave me alone! Who do you think you are, some kind of a preacher? You ought to listen to yourself talk once in a while – our people, our people – why don't you just go on back to 'our people' and leave me alone?" She fled on up the slope.

"Tancy," he called after her.

She pretended not to hear him.

"Hey, Tancy, wait – you dropped your drawers!"

She looked behind her before she could prevent herself, and saw him laughing at her. She ran on.

When she reached the trees at the top of the hill, she was gasping with rage. She halted in the luminous quiet of the woods to calm herself. All was still. He had not followed her. And he had lied to her, the liar: She had not dropped her drawers; they were right there in the tangle of garments. He had deliberately yelled the rude taunt after her because he knew, he knew – what? He knew about her. He knew about her and Jemmy, he knew about her and Sin, it was like he knew every thought she had ever had in all her life. She was glad, oh, so glad that she would never have to face him ever again.

*

The bureau, when she reached it, was closed. They often locked the front door on Sundays. She went around to the backyard. Last night's rain had matted the ashes where the huge three-legged cauldron had stood. The tubs where the women washed dishes had been taken away; only their trestles remained. Evidently they had moved the kitchen indoors for the winter. The yard lay abandoned and forlorn. Where was everybody?

She went in the back door. Everything looked so different – it even sounded different. The long hall echoed under her footsteps. The offices, of course, were empty; she didn't expect to find anybody working there on a Sunday. She took a drink from the familiar water barrel – that, at least, looked the same – and climbed the stairs to the dormitory.

How odd it seemed to be coming back here. She had been away less than a week; it felt like years.

The door to the dormitory was shut. She turned the handle silently, in case Miss Michaels should be napping, and stepped inside.

A gathering of soldiers sitting on the beds stared at her, open-mouthed. Tancy stared back.

One of the men stood up. "Why, it's Tancy!" he said. "What are you doing here, Tancy?" It was Mr. Emory.

"What are *you* doing here?" she demanded. "And where is Miss Michaels?" The men sitting on the beds looked guilty — they ought to; that was *her* bed they were sitting on. Miss Michaels's bed too, and Jemmy's.

Mr. Emory invited her in, as though she were a guest there. "Come in, come in. It's only Tancy," he explained to the others. "Used to be a clerk in the bureau." *Used to be?*

One of the soldiers guffawed and flung a handful of cards onto an upended crate between the beds. The rest began laughing and joking among themselves, relaxed now that the intruder had been identified and found harmless. They had been playing cards, she realized. Playing cards on Sunday, in the women's dormitory.

"Where is Miss Michaels?" Tancy asked again.

Mr. Emory said, "Why, she's went. Went back home, you knowed that, didn't you? Wasn't you here when she left?"

Miss Michaels left out of Knoxford sometime last week, he said vaguely; he didn't know why; and then he said, Yes, he did too know, it was because her mother got sick, but it wasn't that alone: Miss Michaels and the captain had never got on too well, and also, he suspicioned she wasn't too happy about the new cadre that moved in. Mr. Emory indicated the roomful of soldiers.

The men had returned to their card game, slapping the cards down and shouting.

"Where is Captain Dobbins?" said Tancy. "I want to talk to him."

177

"Did you ask for him over at the barracks?" (As though it were usual for her to call on the captain there!) "Aha!" said Mr. Emory, "I bet you're looking to get your old job back!"

"I never quit my job!" Tancy sputtered.

"You can prolly find him there. Just between me and you," he said confidentially, "we got clerks sitting in each other's laps, with this new cadre. Can't harm to ask, though; he might give you your old job back." He turned away to rejoin the card game.

"Just a minute, Mr. Emory. Where is everybody?"

He appeared puzzled. "Well, like I say, ask at the barracks —"

"No, I mean, where are the people? There's nobody out in the backyard. I didn't go inside the jail, but everything is so quiet, the bureau just doesn't look like the same place to me."

"And it ain't; no, girl, it sure ain't. Give this new outfit another week or two and they'll work themselves right out of any job at all. You want it done right, bring in the army, is what I say."

The jail was not deserted, Tancy found when she checked it. A woman lay sick in one of its cubicles and two older women sat with her. Everybody else had gone to the meeting at Eupeptic Springs. To decide what to do when the bureau closed for good.

Tancy said, "But they've brought in all these army people to run the place —"

"Not to run it," said one of the women. "To pack it up and close it down." She nodded wisely, "The word gets around fast. You'll find out."

When she climbed back up out of the jail, she walked through the town and out to the railroad station, for lack of a better place to go. The barracks stood two squares beyond. She could go there and ask for Captain Dobbins, she thought; but what was there to ask? Miss Michaels was gone.

She rested for a minute on the station platform and looked down the tracks that narrowed to a steely point in the distance beyond the lumberyard. What if she waited for the next train and took it to where the tracks ran out? Then took a stagecoach to where the road ran out and then a steamboat to where the river ran out? She had money in the bank and some coins in her secret pocket. She could go where she wanted.

She thought of the boy in *Rollo's Travels* who did that. With his father, Rollo traveled all over, coping with all perils, improving his character, and absorbing the wisdom of his father. How Tancy used to envy Rollo! She pored over his adventures until Billy grew jealous and took the book away and wouldn't let her read it anymore.

But now that she had it within her means, now that she possessed the fare money to take her where adventures began, she no longer wanted to go. Rollo, in the book, had his father to guide and counsel and comfort him. Tancy had nobody. Nobody! Jemmy was lost to her, Miss Michaels was gone; and as for Sin — what sort of wisdom had a mother like Sin to share with a daughter?

A barefoot urchin walking one of the steel tracks windmilled up to her. Despite the autumn chill, he wore only a ragged shirt belted with a string; his skinny, little-boy legs were scabbed and scarred. Like Jemmy's legs. The same impish eyes watching her. "You going somewheres on the cars?" he asked.

"Nowhere," she said shortly. She wasn't going to be taken in again.

He danced forward on the track, showing off. Then his footing slipped. He clawed the air, and before she could save him, he fell spread-eagled onto the gravel beside the track. She snatched him up and looked him over. Nothing more than a scrape, she showed him, and with her handkerchief she gently cleaned his knee.

"That was a bad old tumble, wasn't it?" she sympathized. "That hateful old, slippery old track."

He glimpsed the smear of pink on her handkerchief and began to blubber. Blood! "I want my mama!" he wailed, and clung to her tightly. He reminded her so much of Jemmy, whose bravado invariably crumbled under stress. "I want to go home!"

179

"I know you do, honey. Don't cry, darling. Tancy'll take you home, and Mama will make your knee all better."

She delivered him to the coalyard shack next to the railroad station, where a stout woman with cornmeal on her hands took him in and poured Tancy a cupful of cold buttermilk for her trouble.

"Stay and eat with us," the woman invited. "I don't fix Sunday dinner till I get back from church, and my boarders in there are hungry enough to eat the tablecloth, but I got greens and streak-lean that'll feed one more." Her hands fondled the lad who clasped her knees, careless of the meal sifting into his hair.

"I've already eaten, thank you," said Tancy.

"Whereabouts you stay, dear?"

"Um, Gaither's Mill," said Tancy, to give her an answer.

But back outside, on the station platform, it came to her that Gaither's Mill wasn't such a bad answer. Why not? There was nothing to keep her here now, not the bureau, certainly not Shantytown. She longed for the kindly, respectable people of Gaither's Mill — Stud, good, unappreciated Stud, Swamp, Crazy Nell, and maybe some of the others would have returned as well. She thought of Miss Puddin at her dressing table, with her hair brushed down smooth and golden and shining. "You're my good girl, Tancy."

I want Miss Puddin, she thought, desolate. I want to go home. It was childish, she knew, but she couldn't help that. She was no better than the coalyard boy, as vulnerable as Jemmy.

She shook out her clothing on the platform and knelt to put everything in order. She smoothed and folded all the garments and made them into a nice bundle inside Miss Michaels's shawl. Then knotting its corners together, she slung it across her shoulder and set off for Gaither's Mill.

18

THE TRIP TOOK her the rest of that day and most of the next, walking all the way. At the edge of town the road forked and she didn't know which way to go. She hailed an approaching buggy and asked directions of the driver – wisely, as it turned out, for she met no other travelers for hours that afternoon.

The barren trees allowed her to look about a countryside hidden from her when she left Gaither's. Autumn leaves filled the ditches. The few houses along the road stood vacant; a giant pokeweed poked right through a hole in the porch of one abandoned dwelling. She came to a crossroad that she didn't remember. The small store there had been boarded up, so she couldn't ask her way, but a sign on a pole put her on the right track.

She walked at a good pace, congratulating herself on the impromptu decision to make this trip. What had become of that timorous girl who had so fearfully and secretly fled Gaither's Mill those many months ago? Today she had set out boldly on her journey; she could ask directions, she could pay her own way. She had lost Jemmy, to be sure, and her dear friend Miss Michaels, but she need not allow even these cruel losses to defeat her: She was free.

It was not emancipation that had freed her, she realized; she had had to do that for herself, and she debated whether or not she would have struck out on her own at all, had she not gone looking for her mother. Probably not. Maybe everybody set out, in one way or another, looking for some secret mother.

Now that she thought of it, Sin did the best thing a mother could possibly do for a daughter—she threw Tancy out of the house!

When nighttime came, a family camped beside the road took her in and shared their supper with her, and let her sleep in their wagon under a tarpaulin. She ate bacon and biscuits at their breakfast fire before dawn the next morning, paid her hosts ten cents for food and lodging, and went on, jingling the coins in her money pocket. She had money to spare. Losing the bureau job had hurt, but her bank account in Knoxford salved that wound.

Late that afternoon, following the road that ran beside the depleted creekbed, she trudged around a bend, and there before her eyes, solid against the creekbank, stood Gaither's Mill. She caught her breath. Its stone facade glowed golden in the western sun. The millwheel stood idle, but behind the closed race she could see water in the reservoir, ready for business.

Tancy did not enter to see who might be minding the mill; tired as she was from walking all day, she raced up the lane. Nothing had changed! Here was the canebrake that screened the shallow branch where they caught crawdads; there went the path to the blackberry patch. When at last the house came in her view, she stopped in the lane and looked and looked and looked.

Somebody was sitting on the side porch, where Mas Gaither used to sun himself at this time of the year. It could only be Miss Puddin sitting there in his old rocking chair. The mistress looked up and caught sight of her; Tancy could tell by the way she jerked to attention. She rose to her feet before Tancy reached the gate. She put both hands on her hips and watched Tancy lift the latch, watched her move slowly up the gravel path to the steps, watched her until she finally stood, looking up at her with her head to one side.

Miss Puddin was the first to speak. "I got a beating waiting for you, girl."

It was going to be all right! Tancy flew up the steps. The mistress grabbed her by the shoulders and shook her hard. "Oh, you bad girl! You bad, bad girl!" and somehow they fell into one another's arms.

They were laughing, they were weeping, they were both saying things that neither listened to; and just as well, for nothing they said made the slightest sense. Tancy babbled. The mistress exclaimed and scolded. At last the woman took off her spectacles and with a sigh wiped them on her apron. "Sneaking off like that without telling me."

"I had to. You wouldn't have let me go."

"I would've! I promised you I would! But no, you were always the boneheadedest young'un." She fell to marveling. "I had a funny feeling, somehow, today. We butchered this morning, see, and that was aplenty for one day. I was tired enough to drop, after all the rendering and salting and making headcheese and that; but I had this feeling, I said to myself, I'll just sit out on the porch and shell a few peas — and lo and behold, along you came. You bad girl, you!"

"I'll help you shell the peas," said Tancy demurely.

Miss Puddin sat in the rocker and shelled into the enamel washbasin. Tancy sat at her feet with the dishpan. She told about her job and Knoxford and what it was like at the bureau, and Miss Puddin talked about the drought and business at the mill and how hard it was to get decent help "since the old war."

They shelled nearly the whole bushel measure. The pods were leathery and the peas of poor quality — drought — but they were lucky to harvest as many as they had, Miss Puddin said; peas were about the best they had to eat these days. But when she stood up and said they must go in and see what Patsy had rustled up for supper, she remarked, "You won't say no to some fresh, I spect."

Some fresh. The homely farm words warmed Tancy almost as much as the conversation that had passed between them. She was starved after her long foot journey, with nothing to eat since breakfast that morning.

Already the candle lighted Miss Puddin's place in the dining room. "I usually eat before this late," she said, seating herself. She looked at Tancy standing in the doorway and laughed abruptly. "You might as well sit there." She indicated the other end of the long table. "Things so topsy-turvy, it's hard to know what's right and what's wrong in this old world anymore. Ring the bell, will you. Ring it good. I vow, sometimes I think Patsy's going deaf."

Patsy, startled to see Tancy at the table, juggled her tray of roast pork. She dropped the dish before the mistress with a clatter.

"Bring Tancy a plate and something for her to eat with," the woman instructed.

Patsy rushed from the room, slim of waist, light of foot. Had the baby, Tancy thought.

"She's one of the new help," said Miss Puddin. "It's not like it used to be around here anymore. They come and they go."

Tancy said, "Patsy was here before I left."

"Was she? I can't keep up," she said indifferently.

Patsy brought in a plate and utensils. Her eyes avoided Tancy's as she arranged her place. She brought in mashed potatoes and the gravy boat, she brought in cabbage salad and pickles and biscuits, and the scalloped cut-glass dish that had always been used for butter. A mincemeat pudding waited on the pie safe beside a bowl of custard sauce. Fare had clearly improved during Tancy's absence.

"Well, eat," said the mistress. "I don't want you telling folks I never fed you."

Tancy held her elbows close to her sides, the way Miss Michaels did. She was hungry enough to grab handfuls of the meat; she

184

longed to pile biscuits on her plate and cram them into her mouth. Instead, she took tiny bites, she chewed daintily, with a prissy, pursy mouth.

"Must be quality folks that looked after you," said Mrs. Gaither, "if they gave you the shirtwaist you got on."

"She was a very nice lady," Tancy conceded.

After supper Mrs. Gaither lighted the lamp in the library and showed Tancy the ledgers she had been keeping for the past months. Her meticulous entries marched down the ruled pages and her totals were carried smartly forward. Even with a crop failure, she pointed out, folks still had to get what little grain they made milled somewhere; and with most of the mills around out of commission — well, Gaither's hadn't suffered, if others had.

"They don't hang on like they'd ought," she said. "One bad season, they pile their duds in a wagon and move to town." This wasn't the first drought in North Carolina, she reminded Tancy. Before, folks weathered the dry along with the wet; no longer; and it wasn't only the niggers and poor whites rambling around, it was respectable people you wouldn't believe it of. "Restless," said Miss Puddin, "all of them looking for the easy dollar." She ran a loving finger along her Income column. Her eyeglasses glinted.

"Why, Miss Puddin!" Tancy exclaimed. "I just now noticed you're wearing specs!"

What? The mistress raised a tentative hand, as if to verify that she indeed wore glasses. But of course, she said; she had worn glasses for years; she couldn't remember when she didn't wear glasses.

They were Mas Gaither's old steel-rims; Tancy recognized them. Let it pass, she thought tolerantly.

"I don't know where you want to sleep," the mistress said, when it came time for bed. "Nobody's stayed in Billy's room since he passed — I spect you're used to sleeping in a bedstead now?"

"Let me sleep on a pallet," Tancy said quickly.

There were other differences about Miss Puddin, now that Tancy was beginning to notice. She had worn her work apron to the supper table, and she only took it off when she was getting ready for bed; and she drew large pins from her hair without glancing in the mirror once.

"Let me brush your hair out for you," Tancy offered.

"It's been so long," said the woman, with a pleased laugh. She seated herself at the dressing table. Then she had to get up to start a search for her hairbrush. She eventually located it downstairs, where, belatedly, she remembered leaving it, having dried her hair by the fireplace the last time she washed it.

Could this be Miss Puddin's hair, this stiff, dull mass? "I guess, with the drought and all, you haven't had any rainwater to wash your hair in," Tancy said.

"Oh, I don't bother with all that," said Mrs. Gaither. "I never was vain, you know, like some I could name, setting their cap at anyone wearing pants." She added, as though Tancy should understand the connection, "Elvira Shuford's married again, I don't suppose you'd've heard." A fellow named Overcash, with a gimpy leg. And Prudent had married a one-eyed man, and Pleasant was engaged to a one-armed boy six years younger than herself. It was up to Dilly or Tempe, she said acidly, to provide the family with a whole man.

Long after they retired, the mistress continued to gossip. "You'll want to look up Stud in the morning," she said, with a canny timbre in her voice. "Didn't he used to be sort of sweet on you?"

"No."

"That's how I remember it, from the time you got your growth."

Tancy twisted on her pallet, looking for a soft spot. Sleeping in a bedstead had spoiled her after all.

"There's many a girl be glad to jump the broomstick with Stud, mind you. Any time he comes up to the house, you'll see Patsy waggling her behind at him."

"Didn't Blind Bob come back? I thought Patsy was married to Blind Bob."

"She is. Yes, Blind Bob came back, oh, months and months ago. Patsy figures what he can't see won't hurt him, I suppose."

But Patsy was wasting her time, in Miss Puddin's opinion. A man like Stud didn't have to settle for another fellow's leftovers. And there was a pretty little girl he had been calling on lately at Overcashes'.

"Who?" Tancy wouldn't resist asking.

"Eulalie, I believe Elvira said. Oh, a *pretty* little girl. Got long hair – part Lumbee Indian, Elvira said. Elvira'd like to fix her up with Stud, you may be sure; better chance that way of hiring him off of me." Miss Puddin's voice quickened. "But my guess is, a clever girl like you could catch that fellow before Eulalie knew what was happening to her. Stud was always sweet on you."

Tancy said stonily, "I'm not trying to catch any man."

"A good man, too, Stud is; the way he's looked after Alberta; there aren't many young fellows that good to their mammy." She rambled on about Stud's fine character until at last, lulled by her own monologue, she sounded on the verge of falling asleep.

Suddenly she sat upright in the bed. "What did you do with my silver wedding spoons?" she demanded. "I knew there was something I was forgetting! You sold my spoons somewhere, didn't you? Don't you lie to me, girl."

"I hid them in Billy's coffin," Tancy confessed.

"In Billy's coffin! You idiot! Why did you go and do a fool thing like that?"

"Well, you said for me to hide them and not tell you where, so the Yankees couldn't torture you out of it – "

"Idiotic. Oh, what a stupid idiot." Miss Puddin lay back down. For a while she remained silent. Then she giggled. "Billy's coffin. Well. The Yankees cleaned Elvira Shuford out, did you know that? She had some gold plastered up in a wall beside her fireplace, and the Yankees went straight there and broke into it. It's my belief one of her niggers put them on to it."

Miss Puddin sighed. "The Yankees didn't do much of anything here, dug up the garden a little and lowered one of their fellows down the well, did you ever hear of anything so silly? So my spoons are in Billy's coffin! That was pretty clever of you. It's like having money in the bank, wouldn't you say?"

They were still at breakfast the next morning when Stud knocked on the back door, ostensibly for the day's assignment.

"Told you so," said the mistress, when she came back from talking to him. "He's heard you were here. He kept looking over my shoulder and trying to see you in here. Why don't you go talk to him? He's still out there with Patsy."

"Maybe later," said Tancy. "I want to go visit with all the folks in the quarters."

She stood for a while by herself on the back porch, aching with memories. The very sight of Mas Gaither's old rocker brought tears to her eyes. "Tancy!" she could almost hear him hollering. "Bring me a good cold drink of water from the northeast corner of the well." It was his afternoon joke. He had a morning joke, too, leaving for the barn: "Have to go where I can do some serious spitting." Miss Puddin would not allow him to chew tobacco inside the house. The jokes were over; Mas Gaither, her *father*, was dead.

And Julia had gone for good. Tancy didn't feel like stopping by the kitchen just to see Patsy installed in her place. Blind Bob sat plaiting harness in the doorway, with the baby in a basket at his feet. She pretended not to see him and stepped quickly down the hill.

> *Rain, rain, rain all around,*
> *Ain't gonna rain no more.*

There at least was something that had not changed – Minna's children circling and singing.

I had an old hat with a hole in the crown
Looked like a duck's nest setting on the ground.
Quack! Quack! Quack!

But they turned out to be the children of strangers, singing Minna's children's song. Minna and Risky lived in Shantytown now, Tancy was told. There they had begun a family chair factory, with the children collecting cane, Risky framing, and Minna bottoming. How had Tancy missed seeing them there? She wished she could have talked to Minna.

Crazy Nell had forgotten Tancy. She loped in widening circles away from her when she tried to approach, and wouldn't make friends. Swamp, too, took several moments to place her. "It's all this changing about," he apologized. "It used to was folks stayed where they belonged, and I knowed em all. But now they switch about so, you don't reckonize your ownself hardly." He had grown frailer, slower; he still walked on sticks, although his leg had surely mended long ago.

She looked in on Stud's mother, but only for manners' sake.

"So you come back to the old range?" said the matriarch.

"Yes'm," said Tancy meekly. Something about Alberta made her defensive. Why should that be? Alberta wasn't *her* mother.

"Stud's already got him a girl," the woman said, in a tone of reprimand. "Over at Shufords'."

"So I heard," Tancy managed to reply.

"A real homebody, Eulalie is. That girl can cook up a storm. And sew? She's pieced enough quilts she could set up housekeeping tomorrow. That's how I like to see a girl do, them home things."

"So do I," said Tancy. "If that's what she wants." She sincerely meant what she said, she thought with satisfaction.

"Well, that's what Eulalie wants," said Alberta, offering an argument; but at that moment Stud came panting up from the mill.

189

"Tancy!" he shouted, and flung wide his arms. Under his mother's surveillance, he converted the welcoming hug into a handshake.

"Stud, it's wonderful to see you!" said Tancy; and it was. What a man he was — handsome, powerful looking.

Alberta said, "I washed you a shirt to wear over to Eulalie's tonight, Stud."

"Like to show you the new feed bin we're building down at the mill," Stud said rapidly to Tancy.

"Eulalie's the girl that Stud been keeping company with," Alberta said pointedly. "The one I told you about."

Tancy said mercifully, "I'd love to see the new feed bin, Stud." But you had to give Alberta credit, she thought; she had held their family together and rounded them all up after freedom. That was a lot more than poor old Sin had been able to do.

"There wasn't anybody had grain to spare this year," Stud was saying, "but it'll be different next season, and when they bring it, we'll be ready for em. I look for em to roll in from far as Charlotte to buy our feed."

The new bin rose halfway up the back of the mill, and a crew of four hammered away at the structure.

"You got to put in those stretchers as you go," Stud bawled at the workmen. "Told you that twice already! Now you gotta pull off them top boards and start over." He grumbled to Tancy, "Can't turn my back for a minute." But his voice fattened with pride as he explained his scheme for funneling various feed mixtures into his new bin. In another year, with any kind of a crop, this bin would be too small. They would build another here, and the one after that right behind it; they might double the size of the mill.

She watched his face as he talked. "You really love this place, don't you?" she said.

"Girl, I ruther die than live in Raleigh and em towns. When we come back from Raleigh, and I seen that red clay road going up home there, I vowed I ain't never leave this place again."

She looked up the lane toward the big house and with clarity saw what he did. This pretty place: home. For Gaither's Mill had shaped her life, and his, just as surely as it had any of the Gaithers. You couldn't change that, no matter how the times changed, couldn't ever erase those home years, couldn't cancel out home people. Curiously that revelation gave her comfort, as though she had accidentally touched something infinitely precious. Her fingertips caressed one another. "Like pure silk," she murmured half to herself. "Any girl be proud."

Stud said, "What?"

Emerging from her trance, she said, "Miss Puddin's hair."

"Yeah," he said dubiously, and with a sidelong glance, "Miss Puddin been good to us — give me a raise just last month — "

"Do you remember how I used to go get cold water summers, from the northeast corner of the well?"

Stud said gleefully, "For old Marse! Don't I member? He were a jolly old marse, when he would go fishing with me and Billy. And to the dog races. Me and Billy had to make his chewing bacca for him. Inside the bark of yellow oak was what he liked; we would pull off that fine dark part and fold it and keep it for him; and when he was down at the barn he would chew and spit, and chew and spit. Oh, he could spit clear up to the hayloft. He were some spitter, our good old marse!"

Gone forever, that genial man. "Gone to do some really serious spitting," Tancy said with a smile.

"We got to talk, Tancy," Stud said huskily. "Maybe tonight you and me could talk."

"What about Eulalie?" she teased.

"Oh, Eulalie's — she's like just a friend — "

"Like a friend you're keeping company with, your mother says."

"I don't deny — I don't deny!" Stud wailed. "You got to understand about Eulalie, Tancy! It weren't exactly me, it were my nature – a man's nature. See, I didn't know you was coming back here. If I did, it would been all different, cause of how I always had it in mind about you and me. You got to understand."

She regretted teasing him. Oh, the passion of little boys! Would she never learn?

Why, of course I'll learn! she thought with the delight of discovery. When had she ever failed to learn from the people she loved? Just as Stud had learned from her – sometimes painfully, but then, learning was not always fun. And fun was not always the point.

Still, she had no wish to hurt him. "I do understand, Stud," she said gravely, though inwardly she celebrated what she was beginning to comprehend about herself. "You and I have been through so much together. Wherever I go, I'll never forget you."

Stud looked stricken. "But I thought – but I thought you was claiming Gaither's for home, saying about the well and Miss Puddin like that."

"I was. I do." She groped for some explanation she could give him – and herself. "But there's Shantytown, now, you see."

"You got some fellow in Shantytown," Stud accused. Sweat appeared on his forehead.

"I didn't say that."

"You're getting married?"

"No, I never said that." But she wanted to say something final to end any more misunderstandings between them. What she decided on was, "I know you and Eulalie are going to be very happy together."

*

Tancy walked slowly back to the big house, to absorb everything she could about it, before it began to slip away from her. She paused at the gate where the little dog had sniffed at Billy's hand the day he had come home, a corpse, from the war. Gone, poor Billy. She no longer thought ill of him for the times he assaulted her. Those times were gone too.

The first frost a few nights before had blackened the four-o'-clocks in Miss Puddin's border; chrysanthemums still flared along the fence, but soon they also must yield to the season's grip. Going, going, gone. Standing fenced in the front yard, she could not but feel Gaither's drifting from her, this solid place that had shaped her, that had been her home. ("It's their place, not ours," she heard Henry tell her.)

She went inside the house and asked Mrs. Gaither to tell her what she knew about Lucinda. "Lulu. My mother," she reminded her as gently as she could. "You promised to help me find her."

"I know I did. And I will. But law, girl, what's the rush? I'll ask around. No telling what's become of her, it's been so long."

"She's in Shantytown," said Tancy.

Mrs. Gaither tried not to look flustered. "You don't say! You clever girl, you've gone out and found your mammy for yourself!"

"She's got a house and some land there that Mr. Rankin gave her."

"Rankin. Would that be Hub Rankin, do you suppose? Probably not; Hub Rankin is so stingy, he'd cut a pea in two."

"Miss Puddin," said Tancy sadly, "did you know where my mother was all along?"

The woman gave her one brief defiant look. She wound her hands inside her apron and began to pace the floor. It was for Tancy's own good, she kept repeating. She wasn't ashamed of keeping all that from Tancy. Tancy had been carefully reared, like one of the family, in a good, Christian household, and it was to protect her from just such a shameful life as Lucinda's.

"Mas Gaither called her Lulu," said Tancy.

Mrs. Gaither bridled. "Looks like you know why she had to be sent away." But it wasn't all Mr. Gaither's fault, she said. Any decent woman understood what a man's nature was. No, Lucinda was basically an immoral woman. At Shufords', Elvira had seen that right away and she made the colonel get rid of her. As for Hub Rankin, how poor Mrs. Rankin put up with that going on under her nose all those years, the neighbors never could see.

"And now she's in Shantytown, you say!" cried the woman. "Living in a house of her own. What *sort* of a house, tell me that? Up to her old tricks, I'll wager!"

"She rents out her land, and makes her living that way," said Tancy, and she couldn't resist adding, "She says she'll stake me to a little business of my own in the town."

"Oho. So she can boss you around! You wouldn't want that, would you? When you've got a good living guaranteed you here at Gaither's? I can promise you from sad experience, a girl never grows up as long as she lets her mother boss her. Believe you me, that's what will happen when you move in with Lucinda."

"I wouldn't move in with her. I just want to live closer to where she is."

"Forevermore. Why?"

"Because," said Tancy, "she is my mother."

Mrs. Gaither's face crumpled. She pulled off her steel-rimmed spectacles, turned them over in her hands, put them back on again. "I was more of a mother to you than ever she was," she said brokenly.

It was true. She was. The mother-tie twanged between them like a strummed chord.

"Don't leave me, Tancy." Now Mrs. Gaither was openly sobbing. "I haven't got anybody left. Yesterday, when you came home, I thought – I hoped – " Tears streamed from behind her spectacles. She looked pathetically exposed, she who had always concealed her tears behind her fan.

"Where's your fan, Miss Puddin? I'll go get your fan."

The woman cast about her feebly. "I don't know where it is," she quavered. "Maybe I lost it."

She had owned a dozen or more fans; she never used to be without one; she couldn't have lost them all. Probably she had just stopped bothering, concerned less with appearances as the work at Gaither's Mill interested her more. Weeping, with her hair tumbling down, she looked pitiful and helpless; but Tancy knew better. The mistress had pulled Gaither's back into shape through the cunning of a lifetime. She had reclaimed every one of the workers she needed to run the place. Tancy shivered to think how easily she, too, might be reclaimed.

"I'm so alone." Mrs. Gaither wept into her apron. "I thought when Billy died, I'd been punished enough. Now you say you want to leave me too!" Those were real tears, and instinctively Tancy moved to comfort her. Then she caught Miss Puddin watching her shrewdly from behind the apron, and she burst out laughing.

"Don't cry, Miss Puddin," she said. "Let's enjoy our visit while I'm here."

The woman continued to weep.

"Listen to you!" Tancy scolded. "You'd think I was leaving you forever! I'll be coming back for other visits — maybe next spring. We'll shell a few peas and go look at the baby chickens and the new little pigs, and you'll tell me all the neighborhood gossip." She took the loose pins from the woman's hair and deftly secured the ashy strands. "I'll brush your hair for you, and we'll talk, and it'll be just like old times."

"It won't," the mistress mourned. "You'll turn townified and different and forget all about Gaither's Mill."

Ah, but Tancy was already a different person; didn't Miss Puddin see that? "I'll never forget Gaither's Mill," she said lightly; but her words contained more warning than promise.

Mrs. Gaither blew her nose in her apron, unheeding. "I still claim you, Tancy," she declared. By the time they said good-bye at the gate the following week, the woman had regained her old confidence. "I'll have you back here yet," she threatened.

195

19

A TWICE-TAKEN ROAD, with its reassuring landmarks, trans-
ports the traveler almost as surely as a buggy ride. On her
way to Knoxford, with a mean western wind that had sprung up
in the night to speed her, Tancy marveled that she could ever
have trod these homely ruts with misgivings. When a black
preacher offered her a ride in his buggy, she scrambled in out of
the cold and wound herself in Miss Michaels's shawl. She shared
apples from the bag of Limbertwigs Miss Puddin had sent with
her and listened eagerly to news of Knoxford, news of the fall
elections. Black men sitting in the new legislature — what a world
they were living in!

The light vehicle spun along. They rolled into Knoxford before
the stores closed for the noonday meal. A few shoppers scuttled
along the plank sidewalks, bowing into the gritty wind. Tancy
asked to get down in front of the Freedmen's Bank. Her bank.

*

The padlocked bureau caused Tancy not even a moment's pang
when she hurried past it an hour or so later on her way to

Shantytown. She had left Knoxford heartbroken over Jemmy, disgusted with Sin, in a fury at Henry, appalled by Shantytown. Today, when she stood once again in front of Sin's cabin, she felt healed and whole. *Rollo's Travels,* she told herself. Rollo returning home.

She raised her hand to knock, then changed her mind. She lifted the latch instead and pushed open the door. "Mother? I'm back!"

Sin, standing on a bench, dropped the bouquet of feverfew she had just taken down from the rafters. She teetered on her perch, and Tancy leaped to catch her.

"You like to made me fall!" the old woman shrilled. "Didn't nobody never learn you to knock on a shut door?"

"Not when it's my own mother's door." The word *mother* hung falsely between them; but she owed it to Sin, Tancy decided, and they had better start getting used to it.

Sin's face twitched warily. "I figured, the way Henry told it, you'd gone for good."

"Now, Mother! After I spent a whole year tracking you down?" Tancy touched her shoulder. This little woman was thin, she realized, more fragile than she seemed. I'm stronger than she is, Tancy told herself in amazement. The touch turned into a hug, an awkward embrace for them both, but adequate for a start. "I'm not losing you again, if I can help it," she informed her mother.

Sin glowered at the floor, her lips quivering. "Well," she said, after a moment. "Well, then." She took up the fallen feverfew and removed a few leaves for her teapot. "You can hang the rest of this back with the herbs up there," she said. "I was just fixing to eat my dinner. Potlikker is all."

Tancy jumped to fetch a plate for herself. "Potlikker sounds good to me, a cold day like today."

"You better drink some of this tea yourself; keep you from taking sick."

"You're not feeling poorly, are you, Mother?"

"Chillish, is all. This ornery weather. I knowed I'd ought to put on my flannels yesterday, when the geese begun honking. You got some flannels you can put on? Where's your duds anyhow?"

"I left them with a family in Knoxford. People that run the coalyard down by the railroad station. They fix meals there and take in a few roomers." Tancy took a deep breath. "And I'm going to live there. For a while, at any rate."

Sin struggled to her feet. Furiously she poked at the fire. She lifted the cover of the swing kettle and snarled something unintelligible at its contents. She stamped out the door and stood for a time, arms akimbo, scanning the path. Mumbling, she tramped back inside and seated herself. To Tancy's astonishment, she said mildly, "I don't know but what you're right. I got my ways that I'm used to, and you got yours."

Tancy had come prepared to battle for her privacy. That Sin might cherish her own privacy had not occurred to her.

Sin said, "You and Henry likely to make a match pretty quick, anyway."

"Mother! I have absolutely no interest in Henry."

"Gals always claim that," said Sin. "They ain't any gal but what's looking to get married."

"More like their mother trying to marry them off," Tancy retorted. She spoke the truth, she knew. Miss Puddin's first thought had been to tie her up with Stud; now here was Sin, ready to pair her off with Henry.

"What's wrong with getting married?" Sin demanded. "Us never got the choice, enduring of slavery."

Tancy melted. "Anyway, Mother, Henry has no interest in me."

"Huh! I been watching out for him to come running ever since you got here." She opened the door to scan the path again, and encountered Henry on her doorstep. "There. What did I tell you?" She drew him inside with a triumphant wink for Tancy.

198

Henry rushed to take Tancy's hand. "They said in the town that you were here!" He wore a stiff black worsted suit and carried a bowler hat in one hand.

Sin reared back to mock his attire. "You preaching somewheres?"

"I came over as soon as I could," he said to Tancy.

Sin jeered, "After you got all dressed up."

He finally heard her. He had dressed to go to Salisbury, he explained, to meet with a Quaker lady newly arrived there, who might be willing to teach in the school.

Sin grabbed a bucket and her shawl. "I better go fetch some water now."

Tancy protested. "You haven't finished eating."

"I had all I want."

"Sit down, Mother. I'll get the water." But Sin was already out the door.

"Well, Tancy," said Henry, when they were alone. Account for yourself, his tone said.

"Well, Henry." She broke cornbread into her dish of potlikker.

"It's a treat you're back. I looked and looked and asked everywhere for you. Where have you been?"

"I went back to Gaither's Mill. To see my mistress."

He shifted angrily. "Your *former* mistress."

Tancy tasted a spoonful of soaked cornbread. "This is delicious. Shall I fix you a plate?"

"That Quaker lady in Salisbury," Henry said, already planning, "none of that is decided, Tancy. You can still take over the school here, the way we talked about before."

She allowed him a meager smile. He might crawl right across the table and eat her up, if she encouraged him too much. The lenses of his glasses enlarged those ravenous eyes. But he looked very nice in his high collar, with its drooping innocent bowtie. Not handsome, just very nice; distinguished.

"What do you say?" said Henry.

She thought it through before replying. "I say you'd better hire the Quaker lady."

"You little fool!" He jumped to his feet and paced the floor, swinging his arms. He began arguments that sputtered out before he finished them. He put his hat on and took it off again. He rolled its brim ferociously.

Tancy rose from the table and filled a cup from the swing kettle. "Would you like coffee?" she asked politely.

"No!"

She resumed her seat.

"I mean, yes, if it isn't too much bother," said Henry plaintively.

They sat across from one another sipping their coffee in silence. Whenever Tancy's eyes met Henry's, she was not first to look away.

He said at last, morosely, "I don't know what we're quarreling about."

"I don't know that we're quarreling," she told him.

He opened his mouth to dispute that, but evidently thought the better of it. The room became so quiet that Tancy could hear some trapped insect buzzing, ticking at the windowpane behind the green taffeta curtains. Or was it the sound of her thoughts, buzzing and ticking away? She appreciated this silence; she needed it.

"If I have offended you in some way — " Henry began ponderously.

"No. Sh-h-h."

In a perverse way, she enjoyed his bewilderment. His hungry, perplexed gaze endeared him to her; she really liked this young man a lot, but she dared not let all that energy and ambition consume her.

He said, pouting, "Perhaps I'd just better leave."

"No . . . don't go, Henry." She came around the table and sat beside him. He took her hand, with a sigh of relief for everything being worked out at last.

200

But everything was *never* worked out. Not with Miss Puddin, not with Sin. How could she possibly expect to work things out with this determined, brash young man, whom she had barely begun to love?

She tried explaining to him the importance of her visit with Miss Puddin. She told him about her trip back to Knoxford, and he listened respectfully to her exuberant chatter about the new legislature. When she said she was going to live in Knoxford, not Shantytown, his eyebrows lifted, though he did not comment. But when she told him she was going to ask for a job in the Freedmen's Branch Bank—

"You don't have any banking experience!" he protested. "You don't know whether you'd like it or not."

"That's what I've got to find out."

Oh, it was going to be exciting, an adventure, finding out! The bureau had taught her so much; she had learned a lot even from the few days she had worked in the dispensary, not to mention all the reports and letters she had written, and clerking, handling complaints—

"Teaching," he reminded her.

"Yes, teaching too," she allowed.

"Teaching is what you're best at," he urged. "The school needs you more than any bank does."

"Maybe," she conceded. The sly rascal! He sensed what was most likely to persuade her. If he was so clever, though, why didn't he understand her exhilaration, her feeling of at last *emerging,* and see that she wasn't ready to be persuaded yet?

But evidently he comprehended more than she realized, for he put his arms around her and said with a laugh, "All right, Tancy. Go be a banker, or run for the legislature, or whatever else it is you need to do. Just keep it in mind that I need you, too, and not only for the school. Although I still say you're a born teacher."

"Learner," she corrected him cheerfully. "Think of me as a learner."

Author's Note

The idea for *Tancy* began among the pages of slave narratives, a voluminous folk history collected by the Library of Congress for a W.P.A. project of the 1930s. In that remarkable collection, a reader of the novel may discover the model for the character Jemmy, in a former slave's account of a harrowing separation:

"...his mammy was sold away from him when he was a little boy. He looked down the long lane after her just as long as he could see her, and cried after her. He went down to the big road and set down by his mammy's barefooted tracks in the sand and set there until it got dark, and then he come on back to the quarters."

The slave girl, Tancy, has no such counterpart within the narratives. She is meant to embody the innumerable ex-slaves who set out to find their families after the Civil War. Her yearning and searching parallel what many young people experience even today, looking for some ideal, or "mother," on the way to discovering themselves.

— Belinda Hurmence